A Brighter Day

J Mercer

Contents

This one gets a little bloody and a little gross. I like to think it's campy a la Zombieland, but please enter accordingly.

Chapter One

Vampires Are my Favorite

I peered out my dorm room window as if it were a peephole into the normal world, which it kind of was.

College. Madison, Wisconsin. Day one.

It had been four years since I'd lived this life. A *normal* life. And yet I almost couldn't remember being steeped in it.

Nora was behind me, rearranging her things for the fifth time, telling me she couldn't go anywhere until she was settled.

I was beginning to think this wasn't about having our room in order, but *feeling* settled, something I imagined would take her weeks, if not months. She was terrified of fitting in here. Of making friends.

Riah had moved in yesterday. His roommate had been scheduled for first thing this morning, while Nora and I had gotten

1

the last timeslot today. Riah had avoided his room on the pretext that he was helping us while also giving his roommate space and time with his parents. But the truth was that he wanted us there when they met, for roughly the same reason as Nora was avoiding leaving the safety of our dorm room. They felt like fish out of water. And they were.

He was currently at my desk near the window, shuffling through the pictures I'd printed to hang up in the small space.

"I'm hungry," Nora muttered, turning the music down and spinning to face us from the middle of the small room.

"I'm always hungry," Riah agreed.

"Grace, will you get us food?" she asked.

"So you can hide here and never meet anyone?"

She nodded.

"You're going to have to meet people eventually. Also, everyone's nervous," I pointed out. "Everyone's new."

She bent a little at the waist like she was telling me a secret. "Everyone's not me." Motioning between her and Riah, she added, "Everyone's not us."

"Odds are, there are—"

"Twenty other abnormals on campus," they finished.

With as many students that attended UW, odds were there could be up to seventy-five, but those who grew up wild would never consider attending college, nor would most who grew up in towns like Shady. The abnormal college students would most likely be coming from a life of hiding among normals.

We'd been warned by the current Shady town council not

to look for them. Why they didn't want to welcome any more pacifist families into their mix when they were welcoming wilds and helping them acclimate, I didn't understand. But there was a lot the new leadership did that I didn't understand.

Old Shady believed, along with the governing boards of our species, that we should stay hidden to contain mass hysteria and possible species elimination. New Shady had a more purist mentality, in which they promoted living "pure," which meant letting the wolves and vampires hunt wherever they happened to be, no matter the carnage it might leave behind.

"Okay." I crossed the room to the door. "All three of us are going to meet Riah's roommate, and we're going to ask him to eat with us."

Nora's eyes went wide. "We can't do that."

"Riah has to sleep with the guy, Nora. I think you'll be able to handle a meal."

She shook her head, eyes still wide, and Riah didn't make a move.

"You can do this. Trust me. Anyway, you have to eventually. No time like the present." I opened the door.

The one across the hall was propped open, and a girl sat in view on a desk chair. When she caught sight of me, she jumped up, launched herself in our direction, and skid to a stop right outside our room.

The first thing I noticed was her Vampire Fang t-shirt. They were a decent band, but had a larger following due to how committed they were to the vampire persona—the stereotype, though, so we'd all decided they weren't actually vampires. They just wanted to be.

"Hi! I'm Mai. You should leave your door open when you're home. My mom said when she was in college, everyone left their doors open. She thinks they don't anymore since the pandemic. Which makes sense, right?"

Mai's many braids stopped moving a few moments after she did and I smiled at her. *See,* I deposited directly into Riah and Nora's minds, *she's just as nervous as you two.*

"I walk around naked too often to leave our door open," Nora said from the middle of the room. Then, "What's the pandemic?"

Riah let out a surprised chuckle, which turned into a choking cough, either because Nora just announced she walked around naked, or because Riah was one of the few Shady citizens that cared about what was happening in the outside world.

I knew what the pandemic was because Charlie, my best friend from Chicago, told me all about it. Shady had been spared, though. Maybe something to do with our above-normal make-up.

A new virus killed so many people that pretty much everyone stayed at home for an entire year, I told Nora. *I'll explain more later. For now, pretend you know what she's talking about.*

"Oh! The pandemic. Right. Sorry."

I squinted at her. *Also, do you walk around naked?* Because this wasn't something we'd discussed.

"No, I don't, I just..."

She just didn't want to leave our door open. *Don't reply to me out loud. Just think of me as a voice that... guides you.*

Mai studied Nora with a confused smile. Her stance might have been awkward to a fellow graceful siren, but to Mai, I doubted Nora's nerves showed. She presented as elegant. Swan-like. Her skin glowed—sirens were gorgeous, hands down—and her heavy black curtain of hair was as shiny as could be. Maybe that's why sirens were so much better looking than the rest of us; everything about them was brilliant and healthy.

"I'm Grace," I told Mai, trying to usher us past the subject of nudity. "This is Nora and Riah."

"Wow." Mai strode into our room. "You can see the whole campus from this side. All you can see from ours is the little courtyard." She kept moving for the window, eyes on the view, but as she passed Nora, she slowed and turned to her as if caught up in a spell.

Really, it was just your average siren charm. I could feel it myself, but as often as Stella had used it near me over the past four years, it was fairly easy to pull myself out of. As for Nora, it was only wafting from her because she was nervous. To a siren, as one of our teachers used to say, proceeding cautiously was to slowly ooze charm. They didn't even really need to think about it.

Mai physically shook herself off and gazed out the window. When she turned back around, she caught sight of the pictures in Riah's hand. Nate was currently on top of his shuffle.

"Is blondie your boyfriend?" she asked.

"I'm her boyfriend," Riah said. It read like jealousy, but I knew it was nerves. He held the picture up. "This is her cousin."

Nate's arm was slung over my shoulder in the shot I'd printed of us. I'd chosen it because of his trademark smile, cocky and irreverent all rolled up in amusement. When I looked at it, I could convince myself he was safe, even if he was missing.

Missing from me, anyway. He'd disappeared last winter after I revealed some particularly nasty family secrets and smashed his dad's head into a handrail.

Guess I couldn't blame him.

But the longer no one heard from him, the more I worried. Maybe he was insanely mad at me—dad's head and all—or maybe he'd found his father and they were starting over somewhere new.

My uncle had disappeared the same night my cousin did, he while in custody on the way to the hospital. It was possible he died on the way, that he'd coerced the EMTs to let him go, or that the EMT's had killed him themselves after finding out what he'd done.

It was Shady after all, and sometimes vicious was called for.

Point is, my uncle was a psychopath and Nate had been his errand boy. It's exactly what I didn't want for him, which left me pretty conflicted—hoping I'd killed my own uncle if it would mean Nate was free and getting on with his life.

I slid up closer to Riah as he continued to rifle absently through my pictures, Mai scanning the faces as he did.

Me, my brother Justin, and his vampire wife Clara, taken at

their wedding over the summer.

Christian, Maribel, Aster, and Jeremy—dendrite, vampire, werewolf, vampire.

Ethan, Stella, Riah, and I—vampire, siren, werewolf, dendrite.

Charlie, Mateo, and I—human, human, dendrite. It was a shot from when we were ten, back when I was almost as blissfully ignorant as they were. I'd known what I was, of course, been to Shady on holidays to visit my grandparents and knew of the other abnormals that existed, but I hadn't yet begun to realize the whole—or horror—of what we could do.

I had no idea back then that werewolves could smell emotion, relationships, and illnesses. No idea they were even, loyal souls who could rip your throat out as easily as it was for me to open a jar of pickles. I didn't know that while some traveled to the wilderness for the full moon to hunt animals, others were happy to feast on any human they came across.

I didn't realize back then that a vampire could run faster than anything, or that they could map an area with sound waves. I'd known they bought blood at the blood bank in Shady, but didn't know how opposed wild vampires were to anything not freshly procured from a human.

I'd never seen a siren cry silver sparkly tears, and I didn't know those tears could be mixed with random things to do anything from change the color of your shirt to wipe out your entire memory. I'd never witnessed one of their magnificent tails unfurling when submerged, or heard them speak in their native tongue underwater, or experienced the soothing trance of their charm.

Back then, when that picture was taken, I didn't even know everything of what I would become. I knew only that I'd someday be able to speak in someone else's mind, but didn't know memories, emotions, pictures, or even thoughts would follow. I didn't know there was such a thing that even remotely resembled mind control, or that I'd be able to shock people with my fingertips at will.

I didn't know what wilds were, or purists, or elitists, or even the Hand of Humanity, which we sometimes referred to as the Brotherhood, though we tried not to refer to it at all. I didn't know how evil people could be, or how consumed with power, or how some could so easily take a life. I'd thought the world was a simple enough place.

I'd been young and naïve.

Humans were young and naïve.

Now, I could throw an axe with pinpoint precision and match any one of those other abnormals in a fight. This girl from across the hall? She looked like a bunny in comparison to what I knew we were, and a coldness moved through me, that I'd become what I'd become. Not that it could be helped.

"Have you two been together for a while then?" Mai asked, once Riah's hands stilled.

"Indeed," Riah replied. 'Indeed' was my current favorite affirmative due to the show we'd binged over the summer. I smiled every time I heard it.

"My roommate has a boyfriend in the lakeshore dorms, which is where she's been since the moment she moved in." Mai frowned. Then she cocked her head. "Why are your posters upside down?"

"That's how we do it," Nora replied, and I bit my tongue from saying that was not how *I* did it, but how her family did it. Solidarity and all. "It's a reminder to keep an open mind."

Mai ran her hand along a night sky full of constellations reflecting onto the ocean's surface. Only, because of how Nora had hung it, the ocean was on top.

"What's your sign?" Mai asked.

Nora beamed at her, as if this was a question she finally knew the answer to. "I'm Chinese."

I opened my mouth as Mai made a funny face, but what could I say out loud? *That's not your sign,* I told Nora silently. *Do you know the horoscope? Like, are you a Taurus, Gemini, Pisces...*

"Oh! Sorry. Pisces is the fish, right? I pick Pisces."

"You don't...pick," Mai said. "That's not how it works."

Nora bit her lip and bowed her head, embarrassed.

Mai set a hand on her arm, as if in apology that she'd responded so abruptly. "I'm Black, obviously. And I'd pick Cancer." Her smile was kind and her tone empathetic, and that was the moment I decided she should be our friend.

She dropped her arm as Nora looked up at her.

"I'm actually Gemini, but crabs are too cute, those blue ones are my favorite. Well, vampires are my favorite—"

I choked a little on that, disguising it best I could with a cough. Vampires *were* all the rage in pop culture, though; it didn't have to mean anything.

"Crabs and fish are a good match, right?" Mai's tone was soft and inviting. Whether she was hitting on Nora or just understood how nervous she was, I couldn't tell. But it worked. Nora's face relaxed and her smile opened like a bloom.

"We're going to meet Riah's roommate and then eat dinner," Nora told her. "Want to come with?"

"*Yes*," Mai replied. "My mom said if the doors aren't open, I shouldn't be afraid to invite myself. But I *hate* inviting myself. It feels wrong, you know?"

They walked out of the room as if they'd decided on this plan ages ago, and Mai locked her door.

Riah stood and bent his head to mine. "Vampires are her favorite?"

Vampires are everyone's favorite.

He side-eyed me. "Am I going to lose you to Jeremy again?"

I winked at him, even though most obviously not. Third time was not a charm. Plus, Riah had always been the one, even if it had taken me a while to see it.

Catching me around the waist before I could slip out of the room, he ran his nose up my neck to land his lips on mine. I gave myself a long moment to melt into him, then snatched my keys from the desk and hurried out to catch up with Nora and Mai, who were waiting at the elevator.

"Maybe we should take the stairs," I said, as it was agonizingly slow to arrive. It was move in day, after all, and we were only going up two flights.

Nora turned to me with big eyes. "Why would you ever take

10

the stairs when there's an elevator available?"

I grinned into Riah's shoulder as it finally came, stuffed to the brim. A handful of people and a few carts got off, and Nora made sure to position herself by the buttons. When it stopped on the floor between ours and Riah's, gaining three passengers, she asked everyone where they were headed and insisted on pressing the numbers not already lit up for them.

When the doors opened again, she bounced her way out, turning to give a little wave to those who were still on the "ride," as she called it.

"We're from a very small town in northern Wisconsin," I explained to Mai, but she didn't seem bothered.

Riah's door was propped open and Mai patted Riah on the back for this, like he'd had any say in it. His roommate was stretching sheets onto his bed, looking every bit the star football player his social media announced him as.

When he noticed us, his face broke into a wide smile. "Riah?"

"That's me."

"I'm Owen. Or Wilder. I mean, I'm Owen Wilder, but go by either." He shifted on his feet. "Sorry, you already knew that."

I grinned at everyone's nerves and popped into Riah and Nora's heads again: *See, I'm telling you, it's not just us.*

Nora rolled her eyes to me, as if to say that I shouldn't include myself in that. But I was nervous, of course I was. Nervous about zipping myself back up again, and nervous about how they'd do.

Riah reached out to shake Owen's hand. "This is my girlfriend Grace,"—he nodded in my direction—"her roommate Nora,

11

and Mai, from their floor."

Mai slid over to study the eight by ten photographs he'd hung above his bed, and I swallowed hard as I realized they were stages of the moon.

"What's with the full moon diagram?" she asked. "Are you into werewolves?"

"Into werewolves?" Riah whispered, leaning into me as Nora stiffened on my other side.

Like you're into camping or politics, I reminded them both. *Like Stella's into celebrities.*

It was unnerving how the general public was obsessed with paranormals, as if the truth had permeated their collective consciousness. Charlie had gone through a mermaid phase when we were little, had even begged her parents for a fancy tail for Christmas, even though neither of us had a pool to wear it in. When I slipped up and called them sirens a few times, her mom thought it was because I was reading the Odyssey by Homer. At nine years old.

It was a reminder that humans only believed what they believed, despite evidence to the contrary, so I added, *This is a normal conversation. No alarms to be had. Roll with it.*

"I'm just into the moon," Owen replied, gazing up at the ceiling. "And photography."

"Too bad. I'm all in on the vampires and werewolves. Have you read the Vicious Bites series? So hot. Or Finger Paws?"

"Finger paws?" Riah's tone was laced with disdain and I laughed. Because of course Finger Paws had to be about his kind, and it wasn't as cool a title as Vicious Bites.

"Yeah, it's a werewolf paranormal. Not as hot. Because werewolves." Mai shrugged and I laughed harder because Riah bristled, now caught between being offended that he wasn't as hot as vampires and being terrified that we were even having this conversation.

"I'd read Vicious Bites," Nora said.

"I'll read it again with you. It's so good. I have both the hardcover copies and paperback, because they have different covers. Also because the chest on the main love interest and the face on the heroine are both worth having two of. *Swoon.*"

"Are they both vampires?" Nora asked.

"They're all vampires. A world of vampires. Can you imagine?" Mai linked arms with Nora and headed out into the hall, calling back that she was hungry. "Let's go eat!"

I couldn't hear Nora's response, but Riah was still tense. Turning to Owen, I forced a grin on my face and reminded myself that this was a normal human obsession. It did not mean we were outed. It did not mean Shady was known. It did not mean the Hand of Humanity would be breathing down my neck, once again.

It sure as hell felt like it though. And I wondered how long it would take me hearing about us, in theory, before my heart didn't jumpstart every time Mai cried *wolf.*

With adoration in her voice, of course.

Chapter Two

I Need a Spotter

There was a knock at the door.

Riah launched himself against it with a thud. He put a finger to his lips and I raised an eyebrow.

"Grace?" Owen called through the door. "Do you know where Riah is? We were supposed to go to the gym this morning but he left before I woke up."

Riah shook his head so violently that his hair swooshed back and forth.

You told him you'd go and now you're hiding?

"I didn't tell him I'd go," he whispered. "He said we were going. I can't go to the gym, Grace."

I gave him a look. *You can.* Werewolves were as strong as a bear; he was surely worried about how inhuman that would seem. *It'll be good practice. And the more you practice, the easier it'll be. I'll go with, okay?*

"We're changing," I called through the door, glancing back at

Nora. We were both in pajama shorts and a tee, but they'd do as workout clothes as well as anything else Nora had brought with her. "Be right out."

"Nora's coming?" he asked, a hopeful tone distinct even though his words were muffled.

Nora put her hands on her hips.

"What?" I whispered. "I didn't say we'd go swimming." Which she couldn't do.

She frowned. "It's not even nice for you to say that word."

"Swimming?"

"Ugh." She clucked her tongue. "It just reminds me how thoroughly dehydrated I am. How long do you think I could stand under the shower before someone would think I died in there?"

"Grace, I *can't* go to the gym with him."

I wrapped my arms around Riah and kissed his ear. "You can. You need to. Acting normal is all about downplaying your strengths." Pulling back, I smirked. "Literally."

"It's just not that easy to make it look easy," he whined.

With a laugh, I grabbed my earbuds and keys. "You don't have to make it look hard. You just can't show off."

Of course, when I opened the door, Mai was ready with a gym bag in hand. The thing about your roommate never being around and your belief in leaving your door open was that you heard what was coming and were always ready for anything.

The last couple weeks had cemented the five of us. And Mai's vampire obsession—which was Nora's as well since she'd started reading Vicious Bites—now felt like more of a cover than a threat.

I talked Riah into the kickboxing room with me and was having a hard time not laughing while dodging the bag. I had to keep telling him to rein it in, and he was so frustrated at how little force he could put behind his punches that it was definitely not making anything easier.

When I didn't think his patience could take one more punch, I called it, slipping around the bag to wrap my sweaty arms around his dry, that-didn't-take-one-ounce-of-effort neck.

Shh, I told him in his head while I restrained a laugh on the outside.

He frowned but let me kiss him all over his angry, frustrated face.

You poor thing. So strong it's impossible to be weak, I teased. And this was one of those times, I could tell by the look in his eye, that he would have thrown me on the bed or moved a couch to show off truly how much strength lay dormant in those muscles of his.

Instead, he closed his eyes and took a deep breath in, sinking his nose into my hair. I felt the rush of him breathing out only to inhale again slowly.

NEA? I asked. Non-emotive aroma. The scent of a person behind their emotions. Something that came out more strongly when wet or, in this case, sweaty.

He nodded into me and wrapped his arms around me tight.

My phone rang and Riah let go of me so I could answer it. He headed back toward the weight room where we'd left Owen and Nora, and I followed.

"I miss you!" Aster chirped, before I had the chance to say hello. "But I'm having the best time of my life. Are you having the best time of your life?"

"It's pretty cool, yes."

"It's *way* cool. Aside from the fact that girls are throwing themselves at Christian. Seriously, even the first day when we walked to the bookstore. It's like they were literally tossing themselves in his path. Totally slowed us down. Very annoying."

"No one's throwing themselves at me," he said from somewhere in the background.

"O-kay," she said with a tone that sounded like she'd also rolled her eyes. "Tell me more pretty lies, why don't you. It's so bad, it almost makes me wonder why I've never thought of you like that."

"Maybe you should," I said, pulling her attention back to me. "You'd be cute together."

"Gross, he's *yours*."

"No. He's not." Christian and Riah's sister Maribel had broken up—sort of. Only because of the distance. Or only when there was distance. Something like that. Aster and Jeremy were doing the same sort of thing, but had promised to be completely open about what was happening in each other's love lives while they were apart.

"What'd she say?" Christian asked.

"Is he laying on you or something?" I wondered. "Am I on speaker?"

"No, we're watching Saturday morning cartoons."

"You're what?"

"You heard me."

"What'd she say?!" he asked again.

"She said 'no, he's not.' Call Maribel and stop pining."

"I'm not pining," he said. "I'm not pining, Grace!" he called to me.

"Tell him I say hi. I miss you guys."

"She says hi and she misses us. But me more than you and don't you forget it."

"She would not say that," he said from beneath what sounded like a pout. "She might mean it, but only you would say it."

I grinned. I did miss them. And I loved them. I loved knowing people so well that I didn't have to think about what I did or what I said, what might be taken as weird or what might be taken with ill intent.

"So what about you?" I asked. "Are guys throwing themselves at you?"

"No, I'm too intimidating."

"She's lying." Christian sounded like he was leaning into the phone now. "Two guys on my floor have asked me about her."

"Gross, you almost kissed me. Get away and call her yourself."

"Maybe I will," he said.

"Good. I dare you." There was rustling. Then, "Sorry, I'm back."

"Poor Jeremy's at home pining for you and you're already dating guys on Christian's floor," I teased, shaking my head as my phone started beeping. I pulled it away from my ear to look at it. It was Christian. I ignored him.

"Oh please, we both know Jeremy Holmes doesn't pine."

"Tell her I'm insulted that she won't answer my call," Christian said.

"Oh, watch your stupid cartoons."

"Hey, they were your idea!"

"Sorry, Grace," Aster said.

"Are you apologizing for me?" he asked.

"Did I say you could listen to our conversation?" she replied.

"You can't expect to talk about me while I'm right here and still retain the right to a private conversation."

I nearly snorted as I heard them smacking at each other.

"You did *not* just bite me, Christian Riley. I am so going to kick your ass." And to me, "Sorry, Grace. I have to run. Miss you!"

"Miss you too!" But she'd already hung up the phone.

Her picture lingered on my screen, a shot of her and my cousin Nate. I'd been so distracted with new classes, and trying to help Riah and Nora seamlessly slide into this world, that I hadn't texted my cousin since we got here.

Finding him on my contact list, I ran a finger down the long list of messages I'd sent him over the past few months. They were marked as read, at least, even if not responded to. I figured that was as good as I was going to get.

With a sigh, I sent another: **halloween supposed to be a big party here. come see me?**

I might not be enough of a draw alone, but I had a sneaking suspicion that a party and scantily clad females in sexy witch costumes most definitely were. Hopefully. Anything to lay eyes on him and make sure he was still in one piece. And not too entirely screwed up. Not completely lost.

Somehow, I believed that the part of *me* that was screwed up since I possibly killed my uncle, the part of me fraught with nightmares and self-hatred, would be soothed if I could set eyes on Nate again.

Like, if he forgave me, then maybe I could forgive myself.

Nora and Mai were spotting Owen on the bench press. The three of them had developed into a unit similar to Riah and I, but without the kissing and general making out. Nora was even comfortable enough with them now that she didn't always insist I came with in order to patrol her, which is how she referred to me catching things she misunderstood and relaying helpful hints and warnings via my voice inside her head. This meant Riah and I had some actual few moments of alone time here and there.

Speaking of which, where had he gone? Not only was he still sticking to me like a security blanket, unlike Nora, but his nose generally clued him in to my mood. And when it tanked, or even wavered, he'd slip an arm around my waist and press his lips to my temple.

My mood tanked every time I thought of Nate. Or my uncle.

Instead of comforting me, he was walking directly toward a girl who also had her sights on him. As if they knew each other. She was petite, like Aster and Ava, and her bright, amused smile pressed cute creases into her cheeks.

They stopped one foot from each other, and she looked up at

my boyfriend with big, innocent eyes.

I'd never so suddenly disliked a person. Not even Sofia. And Sofia had been obviously vicious.

I took a step forward, weighing whether or not I should join them. If I did, I was casting myself as the jealous girlfriend, just like Sofia had that day early freshman year.

I trusted him. I didn't need to join them.

But how could he possibly know her? He only knew people in Shady, and if she'd gone to Shady Woods High School, I'd recognize her.

I took another step forward.

"I need a spotter," she was saying. No, *cooing*. "I'm not sure anyone else will cut it, besides you." With a sly smile, she reached out to squeeze his bicep, which wasn't beefy—his strength wasn't about mass—then *winked* at him.

This was when he'd reach for me and let it be known he was my wolf, loyal to the end.

Instead, he nodded. "Of course. No one else *would* cut it." And he grinned.

I'm sorry, what? I shot into his head. Was she some kind of voodoo siren he couldn't resist? But I felt no charm wafting or rolling off her. Nothing that should have this effect.

Delaying no longer, I stepped all the way to them and waited for him to introduce me. But even then, he didn't take his eyes—or his smile—from her.

"Hi." I forced out, offering a hand. "I'm Grace."

"Hi, Grace," she replied, ignoring my hand and not looking

away from him. "I'm enamored."

"Excuse me?"

"I mean." She laughed a little, breaking their eye contact to glance at me. "I'm Aubrin. And I need a spotter."

"Riah..."

He turned the beam of sunshine that was his face toward me, grabbed me in a bear hug, and whispered in my ear. "She's a wolf. She needs me to spot her because..."

Because no one else can spot as much as she can lift.

"Exactly. Isn't that great?"

And then they were walking off for the corner, heads bent together. After surveying the room, they chose the machine that faced the wall and had the worst lighting, making it harder for anyone to see how much they were lifting.

I told myself that, as a wolf, she could smell our relationship. She knew what we were, no matter if she was enamored and he was coming off pretty darn encouraging.

I told myself it made sense. No matter if it felt like she'd plucked my heart from my chest and devoured it like a werewolf would a slab of raw meat.

More than a little salty, I stalked over to Nora, Owen, and Mai, who were now stretching. Today's topic of conversation was not Mai's vampire obsession, but Owen's preoccupation with the moon. He was going on about how it wasn't that the tides came in and out, but that the earth actually shifted beneath the ocean, all because the moon told it to.

"That doesn't make sense," Mai said, nose to her knee. Come

to find out, she was a ballerina, and halfway as flexible as a vampire. This was something she'd have loved to hear, but none of us were planning to tell her. "Wouldn't the earth have to shift all the way beneath it then? Wouldn't the ocean water cover everything as it rotates one way and the water rotates the other?"

"No. The earth rotates around the sun and the ocean is pulled by the moon. So the ocean rotates with the earth—around the sun as well. But on top of that, as the moon rotates the earth, it pulls the ocean toward it, causing the high tide on its side, and low tide on the adjacent sides." Owen was moving his hands—I presumed one to show the earth and one to show the ocean—in a way that completely did not help illustrate his point.

In response, all three of us could only stare at him. Me, with my hands on my hips standing over them.

"Okay, wait." Grabbing for his phone, he searched some NASA science website and set the screen in the center of their little circle. He glanced up at me and patted the spot next to him.

Mai frowned as I dropped to my knees. "Why does the opposite side bulge out like that too?"

"High tide."

"But that's opposite the moon. It doesn't make sense."

Owen offered her a grin and a shrug. "I believe them."

"Maybe you shouldn't."

He snorted a little. "Mai. It's *NASA*."

Nora sighed, offered a dreamy smile, and set a hand over her heart. "The sea and the moon are a symbiotic union, just like the three of us."

"The sea and moon are only two things," Mai said, with a cute pout. Her point, I was willing to bet, was that there were three of them.

I'd started to wonder if Mai and Nora both wanted more from Owen. Or maybe from each other. To be honest, it was really hard to tell sometimes who was flirting with who.

"The earth, the moon, and the sun, then," I suggested. "Definitely symbiotic. The earth needs the sun and moon for light, the moon needs the earth to hold it in place, and the sun... Well, the sun needs something to shine on." I winked at Mai. "If the sun shines and there's no one there to see it, does it even shine at all?"

Nora stretched into Owen, smiling up at him. "The sea is drawn to the moon—always tuned to its pull."

He beamed, like she got him, when really I thought she was just excited to be talking about the sea.

"And the moon is so attached to the sea that the water sets its compass," he said. "It circles round and round and round, unable to untether itself from its orbit."

"Exactly!"

"The earth sets the moon's compass," Mai corrected. "Not to mention, if you ask me, the moon and the sea do not have a healthy relationship. The moon pushes and pulls and the sea just goes along with it. The moon is quite manipulative."

They both looked at her for a moment, then back to each other. I raised an eyebrow.

"Hey!" Owen said. "The full moon is next weekend. Let's take some blankets out to Bascom Hill. Think we'll be able to see it from there? Or the terrace?"

Nora and I shared a look, because Riah couldn't be anywhere near Owen, or this campus, on the night of the full moon.

"We're going home next weekend," Nora said.

Owen's face fell. "Oh. Right."

"Hey, what am I?" Mai asked with a tilted smile. "I'm not going anywhere."

Nodding at her, but still forlorn, Owen agreed. "It's a date."

Chapter Three

Not Dinosaurs

One week later and Aubrin had become our sixth wheel. Or third, whenever Nora split off with Mai and Owen.

I told myself it wouldn't have bothered me if she didn't light up like a lightbulb every time Riah glanced her way.

I told Nora it made sense she'd cling to him—to us. Aubrin had grown up normal in a very small pack, so she was used to this world but not used to being alone.

I told Owen that Riah wasn't being a bad boyfriend. That he and Aubrin had a lot in common. They were both into wilderness exploration and obsessed with the keto diet, which was how I'd started explaining away their preference for raw and rare meat. But on top of that, Aubrin could talk current events and politics with Riah five times longer than the rest of us.

I told Aster, Stella, and Charlie, all separately, that I didn't feel left out when Riah and Aubrin started in on one of these topics that they both loved and I knew very little about.

I told Nathan, who still hadn't written me back, that though I'd worried about Riah wanting too small a life, maybe I should've been worrying that he'd find someone who was a better fit for him if he was exposed to thirty thousand undergraduates.

I told Riah it didn't bother me that he was as protective of Aubrin as he was of me and Nora. The three of us had each other; of course she should have us too. I told him I wasn't jealous and did my best not to smell like it.

I told myself that Aubrin's obvious desire couldn't be that alluring. And I told myself that all the wide-necked shirts she wore, the kind that hung off one shoulder, weren't for him but to show off the two large roses tattooed there.

"Grace?" Owen and I were still at the library, later than everyone else because of Chem 109. We were lab partners and in the same lecture, so we'd bonded over titrates and the need to study more than the rest of them.

I finished the equation I was working on, then looked up at him. He was across the table and one spot over because neither of us had bothered moving when Riah, Nora, Mia, and Aubrin had left. "Yeah?"

"Did you hear Aubrin and Riah talking about camping?"

I had, but I'd been trying my best to ignore it. Earlier, when Aubrin had closed her books and started packing up before the rest of us, she'd struck up a conversation on the subject, orchestrating it to reveal that both her family and Riah's family 'camped' on a regular basis, then going so far as to suggest they plan an overnight together sometime.

Since all this 'camping' happened on the full moon when they weren't safe for outside consumption, Riah, Nora, and I knew she meant just the two of them, even if the Mai and Owen didn't.

"You'd go with them, right?" he asked.

I looked back down at my iPad. "They're not going camping together, Owen."

"If there's one thing I've learned about Aubrin in the past few weeks, it's that she's pushy and tends to get her way."

"I don't camp."

"Grace."

"I'm not worried about it."

"Not worried about it, or not worried about her?" He raised an eyebrow and I saved my work, then turned off my tablet.

"Should we go?" I'd learned enough about Owen to know that when he got chatty, we weren't going to get much more work done. Also, I didn't want to talk about how, on paper, Aubrin was the perfect match for my boyfriend. I was holding onto the fact that he'd been completely devoted to me since arguably the day we met.

We packed up quietly and wound our way out of the library without a word, but as we hit the sidewalk, Owen brought it back up. "If you don't go camping with them, I'll have to. And I hate camping."

I glanced over at him, his face framed by Bascom Hill stretching up to his right. "Riah's not going camping with her. That's not how his family works." Except it had, the one time. Which was how he ended up with his first girlfriend.

29

"You're sure?"

"I'm sure."

"Good. Because camping is how my brother died." Grief cracked open his expression for a moment before he reined it back in.

I gaped at him for a bit, then realized I was gaping at him and pulled myself together. "I'm so sorry." If I lost Justin, it would change me forever. I definitely wouldn't be as jovial a person as Owen, not that I was even that in the first place.

He picked at his fingernail like it was an important surgical extraction.

"Do you want to talk about it?" But of course he didn't want to talk about it. I could kick myself.

Looking up from his nails, squinting at the streetlight ahead, he said, "It ruined everything, really."

"I can only imagine, Owen."

We crossed the street and followed the trees, strung with lights, that lit the way to our dorm. It was after midnight, which was the other reason Owen had stayed with me at the library, aside from the chem pre-lab we had to get done.

"Do you believe in vampires?"

I stumbled. Owen reached an arm out and caught me. Hopefully he read my surprise as a result of the rapid change of subject. "Are we talking like how Mai believes in vampires?" I asked.

"No, we're talking like for real."

"Of course I don't." Because if you knew something was real, you were past the point of believing. There was faith, and then there was certainty.

He folded his arms tight across his chest. "We never got along, my dad and I. I was never enough for him. Not like my brother. But now that I'm the only one left..."

"Owen." I reached out to touch his arm for comfort and because I was confused. "I'm not getting the vampire connection."

He stopped and turned to me at the crosswalk. "My mom's convinced a vampire killed him."

I should have told him that was crazy. My training instructed me to *make them feel crazy*. But under the circumstances, when he was choking out this vulnerable story about his brother dying, how could I attack his mom?

It was nearly impossible to face him, to look him straight in the eye as if I wasn't trying to hide a million things he wasn't supposed to know, so I wrapped my arms around him. He held on tight. So tight. I patted his backpack as he sniffed. This big football player who slept with a Squishmallow.

He pulled away from me to wipe his nose on his sleeve, his frown deep as we crossed the street to our dorm.

"Why does your mom think your brother was killed by a vampire?" I asked, as he scanned his ID card to let us in. Was his mom crazy, or did his family actually know the truth about abnormals? "Let me think back on what I've learned from Mai." I tossed him a soft smile in front of the elevators. "Did he have bite marks on his neck?"

"My mom's not crazy."

"I didn't... I didn't say she was."

31

A plus B equaled C: *My mom believes vampires exist* plus *my mom is not crazy* equals *I believe vampires exist.*

Tread carefully, Grace. Tread very carefully.

"There are plenty of people who believe they're vampires." My words came out choppy. I took a deep breath, trying to center myself so I wouldn't sound suspicious. "People who drink blood and avoid the sun and pretend they can't look at a cross. People who shave their incisors to points or get veneers. I wouldn't be surprised if those people went around biting people too. Maybe even killing them and drinking their blood."

Owen only studied me, which caused the hairs on the back of my neck to stand up. What had I walked into here? Could his family actually believe in us? Could they actually know about us? Were we not as under wraps as we all thought we were?

"If vampires are real, then are dinosaurs too?" I tittered a little. *Tittered.* Gah, I needed to get control of myself.

"Not dinosaurs," he said as the elevator doors opened.

I stepped in, my heart pounding out the heavy thrum of a scared dinosaur running from a T-Rex. *Not dinosaurs.* Did that mean he believed—no, *knew*—that something besides dinosaurs existed alongside vampires?

As Owen stepped into the elevator beside me, I studied the numbers across the top of the door and wondered if I should press him for more information.

But no. For all the things I'd pressed in my life, always pushing to uncover the truth and make sense of things, this felt too dangerous.

We were silent until I stepped out on my floor, feeling like I'd failed him. Like I'd let him down. Like I'd called him crazy. Which I'd been careful not to. But...

It didn't matter. I couldn't stay for more of this. "Night, Owen."

"Night, Grace." And the doors closed on him.

Shit.

For once, thank goodness, Mai's door was shut. Slipping into our room, I found Nora on the futon, asleep with her feet in a basin of water. The light was still on and Riah was in my bed, scrolling through his phone. He did this sometimes, walked home with her and waited for me to say good night.

And thank goodness he had tonight, because I wouldn't have called him down here on the heels of that conversation. It would've been too suspicious. But the news was also bursting out of me and he was the first person I felt I should tell.

He needed to know what he was up against.

Even so, I didn't know how to say it. What would he do once he realized his roommate was on to us?

Riah swung his feet down onto the floor and popped up to a sitting position, hitting his head on the top bunk. At the thunk, Nora startled, sloshing some of the water out of the basin onto the floor.

Riah's nostrils flared as he studied me. "What happened?"

Dropping my backpack, I shared the memory with them.

As my conversation with Owen finished unspooling in Riah's mind, the phone in his hand slipped onto the floor. "I have to request a room change."

"No," Nora said. "Owen's a teddy bear. He didn't say he hates them or anything. And he said nothing about werewolves."

"He thinks a vampire killed his brother! How could he not hate them?"

"His mom thinks that," she pointed out.

"Why are you defending him?"

"Because it's Owen. He's not going to kill you in your sleep."

"I can't live there, knowing he knows but not knowing how much he knows."

"If he stopped trusting you, wouldn't you be able to tell?" I asked, squatting down in front of him. "Don't you think it's more a red flag if you suddenly, now, right after we had this conversation, ask to switch rooms?"

Nora straightened her shoulders and a soft, gentle breeze of charm floated over to us. Leaning into it, Riah nodded at her.

"Stay here every night," I suggested. "Or at least until you're more comfortable."

"Sure," Nora agreed. "I'm okay with that. We have an extra bed."

Riah and I both looked at her. She did sleep sitting up most of the time, feet immersed in water, but...

"Sorry," I said. "I should've asked you first before I offered."

She shrugged and a smirk slid onto her face. "I kind of figured it'd happen sooner or later."

"And when I'm not here?" Riah looked back to me. "How do I act? What do I say?"

"You act the same and you say nothing. He doesn't know anything about us."

"And he loves us," Nora added. Which was pretty clear. He was as devoted to Riah, Nora, Mai, and I as a werewolf would be to his pack.

I gasped. "What if he's a werewolf?"

"He's not a werewolf," Riah said, tugging me down next to him and burying his face in my neck. He breathed in and out, slow and steady, trying to calm his nervous system. "I'd smell it," he murmured.

Nora gave me a look. "Like you smelled Aubrin?"

We collectively rolled our eyes.

"Oh." Riah pulled his face from where he'd burrowed into me. "We need to tell Aubrin."

"Do we?" I asked.

He grabbed for his phone. "She'll have a better idea of what people in the normal world believe. If this is more common than we think it is."

My skin pickled. "Is this because of Aubrin's camping conversation? Do you think she tipped him off?" Had he been baiting me for information? "What if his brother died hunting?" Which happened, when you were a werewolf. Not often, but it did. "What if his brother was a werewolf, and he's a vampire?"

"I'd be able to smell that too," Riah said, glancing up from his phone.

"What's Aubrin saying?" Nora asked.

"She's on her way."

"She's what?" I snapped. "It's like... after midnight."

"I'm not going to text any of this."

Riah stood to pace and Nora gave me a look, then dried her feet and went to empty her water basin. When she returned, she put on Portishead, which she considered chill music, then snuck back out to refill her water bottle.

I tucked myself back on my bed against the wall and pulled my knees to my chest. That's how I felt about Aubrin coming over.

Before Nora got back, there was a knock on the door. Riah peeked out as if we were doing beer bongs and it was our RA, then snuck Aubrin in like we were on a top-secret mission. She even stood at attention as she glanced around the room, and for the love of all that was holy, she could've changed out of her pajamas or at least put on a bra—her top was so thin it might as well have been mesh. Not to mention it was nearing the end of September, in the middle of the night, and she wasn't wearing a coat. Yet somehow, she had time to paint a full face, as my grandma liked to say.

"What's going on?" she asked, voice husky and soft, as if she thought there was any chance this might be a late-night booty call. In his girlfriend's room.

I don't know why I ever doubted myself. This girl clearly wanted in my boyfriend's pants more than she wanted a safe place to land or any new friends. Me and Nora being the new friends. The three of us being the safe place to land.

For a moment, I considered staying hidden and watching this play out—it wasn't my finest moment, I get it—but then Nora burst back in the room, ramming the door into Aubrin's back.

Aubrin tumbled, rather purposefully if you asked me, into Riah, catching herself by wrapping her arms around him.

I mean, honestly.

Nora apologized before climbing to her top bunk, and I scooted out from where I was sitting to make myself known.

Aubrin took a step away from Riah and tucked her hands behind her back. Which wasn't much better, considering the top and the bralessness and the cold fall wind.

"Grace." Riah turned to me. "Show her."

I raised an eyebrow at my boyfriend for being so oblivious, but did as I was told.

Once the memory ran through my mind and into hers, Aubrin nodded decisively, then guided Riah to the futon and sat him down. She knelt in front of him and put her hands on his knees. "It's going to be okay," she told him.

The balls of this girl, I muttered to Nora, who grunted from the top bunk.

"We thought you should know," Riah said. "And also, is this common? Do people... believe?"

"Yes," she said firmly. "But not in the way you think. Not in a way that should worry you. People want so badly to be a vampire or a werewolf that they drink blood and howl at the moon. I heard about this one guy who stole blood bags from the transfusion site he worked at. Or they buy it on the black market, which isn't even real blood. There's simply a demand, so someone came up with something they could pass off as the real thing."

I'd pretty much said as much to Owen, but Owen had not bought it. And though I was happy it was easing Riah's anxiety, it wasn't easing mine. Because Owen didn't think people just played the part.

He and his family believed. Without a shadow of a doubt.

Chapter Four

Homecoming

We told Owen and Mai we were going home for homecoming, but the truth was that Shady didn't have one, since so few people left in the first place.

As we pulled onto the gravel road behind Jeremy's family's truck stop, the thick woods that made it feel like you were on someone's driveway and not a real road had me rolling down the window to smell the pines. And as the gravel gave way to pavement, I relaxed in my seat, feeling at ease in a way I hadn't since we'd left.

Until we came upon an ugly metal building in a clearing that didn't used to exist. Cutting a hole in the forest to deposit a monstrosity in its place felt like a Sentinel move to me.

And sure enough, five Sentinel stepped into the road, barring our way, no real warning at all. No signs, no waving us down, just sauntering out into the road, trusting we'd stop. Riah had to slam on the brakes.

One walked to the back end of the car, one approached Riah's window, one came to mine, and one to Nora's. The fifth stayed in front of the car.

"License, please," the one at my partially rolled down window said.

"I'm sorry?" Riah asked, rolling down his as well.

"You know," I said, digging into my backpack, "if we were actually human and took a wrong turn, this would not help keep Shady under wraps."

"License," said the guy at Riah's window, while the one at Nora's tapped on the glass.

Riah rolled it down for her with the driver's side controls while she rummaged frantically through her purse.

"It's here," she muttered. "I know it's here." One by one, she emptied everything out of her purse onto my back seat. As she peered into her empty bag, I scanned the pile and reached back to grab it from under her checkbook, then handed it over to the Sentinel waiting.

The guy by Riah reached in and took my keys out of the ignition, then asked Riah to pop the trunk.

"Do you think we're smuggling someone in?" I asked.

"Pop the trunk," he repeated.

Riah did as instructed, then got out to watch the guy poke around under our bags. I wondered if the keys meant someone had previously tried to run one of them over. It sounded like something Nehemiah might do.

When he finished, and Riah moved to slip back into the car,

they stopped him.

"Sorry sir, but to get your keys back you need to submit to a body search."

"A what?" he growled.

The Sentinel stood a little taller. "I need to frisk you. It's standard."

"It wasn't standard a month ago."

"Things change," the woman on my side chimed, opening my door. "You too."

"What are you looking for?" I asked. What could they care about us bringing in? Or was this more to antagonize those who left and returned?

I got out and faced my car, spreading my arms and legs for dramatic flair. Riah snorted but did the same, and our eyes caught over the hood as they patted us down. When it was over and the Sentinel handed me back my license, I let loose with a few sparks. They hopped and skipped across the plastic to her fingers and she drew back as if she'd been bitten.

"Oops! Sorry!" I feigned sincerity. "It's just a little nerve-wracking getting patted down like a criminal."

Her slap stung my cheek before I could even register her hand moving.

Vampire fast. Right. We weren't at college anymore.

I scoffed at her in disbelief, rested my hand against the sting, then slipped back into the relative safety of the car. Riah started to launch himself over the hood at her, but the Sentinel on his side caught him in time and held him back.

I'm perfectly capable of fighting back myself if I want to, I reminded him while holding my shaking hands still in my lap. *But I'd prefer to just get out of here.*

Ripping the keys from the guy's hand, Riah slammed the door as if one of their fingers were hopefully in it, then peeled away in a manner that suggested he'd rather be giving them the middle finger.

"It's over," I told us both, staring ahead to search out the windshield for the familiar. For everything that was still the same. It *was* over, at least until next time. But next time, I'd behave.

Riah was gripping the steering wheel so tight his knuckles were white. "I'm going to tear her throat out."

"You're not."

"Then I'm going to get her fired."

"And who would fire her for that?"

"I don't know. Your brother?"

"Riah."

"I know, I know. I just..." He looked over at me, his eyes narrowing quickly. "You have a mark."

And a sting, but I didn't say it. I also refrained from pressing my cold palm against my cheek to cool the burn, lest he lose his mind. "So I have a mark." I shrugged. "It's still over."

When he pulled up in front of Nora's house, she didn't make a move or a peep. I twisted to find the contents of her purse still scattered across the seat, and a few things had fallen to the floor during the drive. Her license was still in her hand and she was oddly immobile.

"Nora?" I asked.

Her eyelids fluttered and she met my eye.

"You're home." Reaching down to pick up the lip gloss and pen off the floor, I handed them to her.

She blinked and gathered her things, then ran up her walk without looking back.

—— ✍ ——

My mom had never been more excited to see me.

We spent the afternoon in the kitchen, catching up. I'd called home since I left, of course, but most of our contact had been via texts and memes, and now I had the time to describe every little thing.

I missed my mom. I missed my room and my house and my dad and my friends and Shady. Even as it was, I missed Shady like I'd never missed Chicago.

My mom announced she should get started on dinner just when Justin and Clara swept in the front door, and my brother drew me into a hug.

"How were the Sentinel coming in?" he asked.

"That new headquarters of yours is obnoxious," I muttered, for everyone's sake. *One of them slapped me,* I told only my brother and his wife.

Justin pulled back with a raised eyebrow and shared a look with Clara.

"It is a bit obnoxious," Clara said, squeezing my hand as she

43

moved past us to help my mom with dinner.

My brother cleared his throat. "They had to put us some-where, now they've let the cops back into their station." *Did you mouth off?*

I tried to control my sneer. *As if that makes it okay?*

He only stared at me.

Fine, I might have shocked her a bit.

A smile grew on his face and he brought me in for another hug.

After last year, when the Sentinel had tried their inexperi-enced and uneducated hand at policing, allowing a monster to snag dendrites for experiments (my uncle, he was that monster), they'd been relegated back to their original purpose of screening the wilds coming in and keeping an eye on who left town to hunt the surrounding communities. Because the one thing everyone agreed on was that we couldn't have a trail of dead bodies leading back to Shady Woods.

They'd been formed to protect the town from threats. Not college students. My brother and Clara had signed up for that, in the beginning, and stayed because they believed it was important to have people on the inside. Plus, they were committed to the long haul. Or, hopefully, the eventual overhaul.

"Things might seem worse," my mom said, "but the fact that the new council and the police force can meet and work in the open, opposite the new council and the Sentinel, means progress."

I slid onto a stool to watch them cook. "Two governing bodies with their own respective police forces, both trying to control town, sounds like a recipe for disaster."

"You've gotten quite cynical at college, then?"

"I was pretty cynical before we left," I admitted.

My mom frowned at me. "After dinner, we should take a walk out behind the neighborhood. There's a whole new development to accommodate all the wilds who've embraced our way of life. They're on our side—living and working and going to school."

"Ah, yes, the joys of double permitting," Justin muttered.

It took me a minute to figure out what he was saying. When I did, a small laugh escaped me. "People have to apply to both town councils?"

"If you want to be safe," my mom muttered, "you even have to pay property taxes to both councils."

"A small price to pay to have Old Shady back," Clara said, pulling out a cutting board.

My brain was starting to hurt, but tonight was supposed to be about family. No Owen, no town problems, just a full moon night in.

"You know what?" I asked. "Can we actually *not* talk about it?"

My dad and grandparents burst through the door with bags of my favorite snacks, and my mom smiled.

—ele—

Aster had taken the idea of Homecoming and ran with it, creating a new group chat and requesting we each choose one thing we wanted to do while we were back in Shady.

She and Riah were unavailable Friday night, of course, due to the claws and teeth and general hunting obsession, but Saturday she considered everyone's choices and created a schedule.

Nora and Christian opted out. Nora because she wanted to spend as much time as possible underwater in Iara, and Christian because he'd signed up for a volunteer shift at the blood bank and planned to get up early to feed all the animals in the basement of his father's clinic beforehand. Like the do-gooder he was. Showing us all up.

For the rest of us, the first stop Saturday was the grocery store. More specifically, the specialty cooler hidden in the back storage room. Riah and Aster wanted to load up on all the delicacies they didn't have access to in Madison or Minneapolis, then Riah's parents were going to cook them for us for dinner.

I'd never been in the cooler before, since dendrites weren't in the market for the kinds of things the town hid on the off chance a normal got past the truck stop. And needed a grocery store.

When I put it that way, I could see how Old Shady was a bit paranoid. But better safe than sorry.

Stella went straight for the wall of aquariums that held seahorses, urchins, and a plethora of seaweed varieties, while Ethan and Jeremy stood with their arms crossed in front of neatly stocked canning jars of various animal bloods. Riah picked up a cellophane wrapped package of elephant ears as Aster went for a watery freezer bag of crocodile tongue, and I scanned the labels:

46

Quartered head, Feline.

Brains, Ovis Aries (Domestic Sheep).

Heart, Panthera Leo (Lion).

Hamstring, Homo Sapiens.

I recoiled, stumbling back into Aster. "I'll be... I'll be outside." I gulped in a breath of air that now only tasted like human flesh, damn my imagination, and ran for the door.

Pushing out of the back room, I doubled over by the dairy case, studying the neat rows of butter to bring me back to sanity. It felt like my whole body was shaking but my hands were the worst, and I was certain if I didn't get a hold of myself, I'd faint right there. I'd probably fall into the eggs and then have little dirty birdie fetuses to contend with.

The thought didn't do much for my retching stomach, so I focused again on the butter and put a hand under my shirt, directly onto my belly to try to soothe it. My other hand went out to brace myself on the dairy case but someone caught it before it could land.

A warm hand and another to my elbow.

I looked up.

"You okay?" Nehemiah asked. He was what had counted as trouble when I'd moved here, before trouble had actually swept in.

"No."

His hands were strong and steady and warm, and he helped me right myself.

"You need me to beat someone up?"

I let out as much of a laugh as I could muster. "No, nothing like that."

"You were in the cooler?"

I nodded.

"They've sold human meat in there for a few years now."

"I know." I'd heard the rumors. "I'd just never seen it before." Which, come to find out, meant I hadn't really believed it. Why had we allowed anyone who would sell—or buy—human meat into our town? I know humans weren't technically one of us, but the whole point of Shady was to protect them. From us. Right?

I pulled my elbow and hand from him, and for a moment, our very short dating history was a whole lot of awkward. "My imagination can take it, I guess, but actually being faced with it is something else entirely."

"Yeah, I hear that."

I made a question of my face.

"I didn't last long out there," he explained.

Ah. He'd been trouble in high school because he was always wanting to leave, to explore, to be a hero in the normal world. He must have tried and, well, here he still was. "I'm sorry," I said.

He shrugged. "You were right. It wasn't easy. How's Riah handling it?"

I frowned. "Fine? He seems okay."

Nehemiah laughed a little. "You haven't asked him?"

"I mean, we've talked about it." But had we, before this recent situation with Owen? Had I ever actually asked him how he was adjusting—how he felt—before that? Or had I just assumed?

"Sure." Nehemiah studied me with a small smile, like he could smell there was more to my answer than I was giving him. Which he could, because he was a wolf.

Okay, the second thing I didn't miss about this town was how a quarter of the population knew exactly what I was feeling. And half the time, they knew it better than I did myself.

"Well, thanks for that," I muttered. Because worrying I was a crap girlfriend had effectively booted the meat cooler right out of my mind.

I couldn't stop thinking about it the rest of the day. Not during our axe-throwing session, which had been my pick, and not as we huddled around the Jenkins' kitchen island, trying unique meats.

By the time everyone else had left and I was helping his mom do dishes while his dad wiped down the counters, I had a plan.

"Mr. Jenkins, when are you taking Riah and Ava to the Apostle Islands next?"

Riah stopped eating, the last crocodile toe halfway to his mouth. This was the way he helped clean up. By eating whatever was left.

"February. It's quicker across the lake when it's frozen."

I took a pot from Riah's mom to dry it and asked her, "Haven't you ever wanted to go with? See the ice caves and the sled dog races? A family vacation of sorts?"

Being a good girlfriend meant seeing all the parts of Riah's life. Aubrin might make more sense on paper simply because she'd been there and I hadn't. Maybe I'd develop some crazy obsession with the wilderness too, if I gave it a try. Who knew? I'd started as a city girl.

Of course, Riah would never let me come with if I was there alone, but if I had his mother and sister at the hotel with me? Vampires who had my back? More likely.

He narrowed his eyes at me. "Abnormal families don't go on family vacations."

"Maybe they should." I focused on his mom, not the alarm in his voice. "Everything else is changing around here, why not that too?"

"No." Riah's face was gaping a big fat *hell no* at me.

I shrugged. "Just an idea."

His mom set her hand down on the sink. "Okay. I'm intrigued. What did Clara do about her blood source when you all went to Chicago last year?"

"She brought it with. The hotel had a fridge and a microwave."

Leaning against the counter, she studied me, or maybe it was the idea she was studying. Mr. Jenkins only looked kind of amused, and I took that to mean it wasn't the worst idea in the world. At least, not as dangerous or horrifying as Riah's face was suggesting.

His mom picked up the last pan she had to clean. "And I suppose if we went on a family vacation, Riah might ask if you could come with?"

"No!" he cried. "I would not!"

I nodded. "I'd think, wouldn't you?"

She laughed. "It doesn't really sound like it."

"You know, sometimes normal families vacation together. And if you were going to ask another family to come with, you'd probably ask my parents, right? And then my parents, well, they wouldn't leave me behind."

"Grace!" Riah slapped the last elephant ear down on his plate.

His mom laughed and looked to Riah. "You've got your hands full with this one."

"Mom! You can't seriously think this is a good idea."

"Actually, I kind of do. I don't know why I haven't thought of it before. A family vacation?" She winked at me. "How very pleasant."

The wink confused me. Was she just playing along or had I really managed to start something here?

"I cannot believe you." Riah shook his head at me and left the room.

I gave him a minute, finished up drying the dishes, then found him in the living room. He was standing between the couch and coffee table, as if he'd meant to sit down but hadn't gotten that far. Setting my hands on his waist, I turned him around, then pulled him to me.

Really, it was more like I pulled *at* him, which caused me to stumble forward into him, as he was frozen to the spot.

"I don't want you near me when I'm like that, Grace. You can't understand what it's like."

I tilted my head. "I can't understand what it's like to feel like a monster?"

Riah took a sharp breath in. So I knew him well enough to

51

know that, at least, that he was ashamed of that side of him. Did Aubrin? Was she ashamed?

"I won't be near you when you're like that," I reminded him. "Just before and after."

"That's close enough," he grumbled.

"I've been there, when you almost turned, remember?"

"Why are you doing this?"

I stared at him, at his beautiful brown eyes and that face that made me ache a little when I studied it. "I don't want Aubrin to be the one who goes hunting with you."

His brow furrowed. "This is because you're jealous?"

"No, that's not what I mean. You came to live normal for me. And I ignore this big piece of you, all the time. I don't talk to you about it, and I don't know it."

"I don't want you to know it. That's the point."

But Aubrin knew it. Still, it wasn't about being jealous. Or it wasn't about her, anyway. Jealous she understood that part of him in a way I couldn't, maybe.

"It's half of you, and it feels like a secret you keep from me," I explained. "I just want to know you the best I can. And maybe you thought I couldn't handle it before, but I can now."

"You do know me the best you can."

"No, I don't."

He growled in frustration, his chest rumbling against mine.

"Just think about it, okay?"

"Not sure why I need to. Seems you've got my mom thinking about it."

I bit my lip to keep from smiling about how well that had gone. "It's not like anyone in the houses or hotels of Bayfield are at risk. And I know to stay inside."

He sighed. "I'm afraid you'd be a honing beacon, Grace. That my nose would want only you."

"You think... you think you'd run all those miles across the ice to find me, even if I was far enough away you shouldn't even be able to smell me?"

"I don't know, okay? I just don't want to take the chance."

"Riah, that would be very... human of you, wouldn't it? Too human, for the full moon. And could you even make it in time?"

"It's not worth taking the chance." But his words were weaker now.

"I don't think that's how it works, but ask your dad, okay?"

Settling his forehead against mine, he wrapped his arms around me and I wondered over his shame. Shady was supposed to be the one place he was truly accepted, but still, he couldn't accept himself. Did that mean it had something to do with me?

Aster wasn't ashamed, but then she hadn't known me when I'd first walked into town. She hadn't known how fiercely protective of humans I'd been, and she hadn't seen how much I hated myself for being abnormal.

If I'd done this to him, then I needed to be the one to undo it. I needed him to see that I accepted him completely.

Maybe I hadn't always, but I did now. I was in this life to the end.

Chapter Five

Don't 'Dude' Me

"Tell me one more time why we're here?" Nora asked, as we stood in front of a house that both noise and people spilled out of.

It was a Thursday night, and Owen had heard about this party from some random guy in one of his classes. It seemed that this was what was expected of you, if you wanted to act normal in college—going to parties you'd heard about but weren't technically invited to, even if it was on a school night.

We'd been very committed to acting normal over the past month, ever since my conversation with Owen.

"Don't worry. Owen and I have your back," Mai told Nora, squeezing her hand. The three of them had walked here linked, Mai to Nora to Owen, which meant Aubrin kept trying to grab for Riah's hand, the one that wasn't holding mine.

Thankfully, he'd eventually tucked it into his pocket.

"I'm not nervous," Nora said, glancing back to Riah and I. "How do you know I'm nervous?"

Owen nudged her, a cute smile turning his natural pout. "You always look at Grace and Riah when you're nervous. Did you not drink in high school?"

"Not alcohol," Nora muttered, looking down at the sidewalk as if she were embarrassed. Mostly, Shady drank siren tear concoctions. "It's so dehydrating."

Owen grinned. The two of them had bonded over electrolytes.

As Mai and Owen took to the front steps, Nora sagged behind. A siren was set to take in stimuli from a muted, underwater environment, which meant out of the water everything was that much stronger. And Shady was pretty quiet compared to Madison in the first place. Living there for four years must have recalibrated me too, because same as Nora, I had to brace myself against the pounding bass as we entered.

People were everywhere, but a guy wearing a pink, rainbow-colored shirt with a unicorn on it pointed us downstairs where the beer was and where "the mess could be made."

My first observation, as we descended into the basement, was that house parties were like crowds on steroids. Not only tightly knit and jostling against each other, but with arms thrown up here and there from where people danced inside their own little pockets. This seemed to mean that Aubrin felt she could writhe against Riah while chatting with Mai, as if she wasn't intentionally rubbing against him. No matter how many times he stepped away, she kept eventually finding her way to his side.

I nearly pulled out my phone to message Sofia that I missed her. That she'd been a respectable enemy, that I appreciated how up front she'd always been about her nefarious intentions, and that I now cherished the time we'd spent together.

As if I'd manifested it, my phone buzzed in my back pocket and I slid it out to see Nate's name on my lock screen.

I froze in the middle of the pulsating, sweaty crowd and stared at the first sign of life since my cousin walked out of that abandoned house last year: **hey good lookin.**

Nate! Hi!

As I waited for his response, I elbowed Riah and showed him my phone. His eyes softened and he smiled; he knew what this had been doing to me, and he knew about the nightmares.

So eager, little beaver, he replied.

Where are you? Can I call you? Not from here, I couldn't. Not from this basement. I elbowed through the crowd to get to the stairs.

I watched my phone as I went, but he was no longer typing. Please tell me I hadn't lost him. The thought woke me up at night, that he'd turned into something rotten like his dad, or that he hated me with everything in him.

"You really shouldn't keep your location on." The soft drawl reached my ear as I hit the first step, sending a shock up my spine. I stopped hard and looked up.

Nate.

Standing directing in front of me, on the second step, with that skeezy grin on his face.

Tossing myself at him, I wrapped my arms around his waist until we nearly tumbled back onto the stairs. Catching the railing, he kept us upright.

"I was worried about you," I muttered into his shoulder, a crest of emotion nearly bowling me over. I was pretty good at compartmentalizing by now, but every so often my fear and horror and rage bubbled through.

"Worried about what?"

Worried about everything. I was so relieved to see him. So relieved he was smiling at me.

"Hey." He pulled back to look at me. "I'm good, okay?"

"And you don't hate me?"

"Would I be here if I hated you?"

I squeezed him close one more time, wanting to ask if he knew where his dad was, if he knew whether or not he was alive—if he knew whether or not I'd killed a man—but I couldn't get the words out. Not here. I didn't think I'd be able to have that conversation without sobbing.

"You and Riah okay?" he asked.

"Yeah, why?"

He nodded toward where Mai, Nora, and Aubrin were dancing; Aubrin doing so right in front of Riah, clearly putting herself on display.

She has a thing for him.

Clearly.

And she's a wolf. Which means, unfortunately, that Riah can't get past the loyalty and pack mentality.

Nate raised an eyebrow but I wasn't ready to face what he meant by it. Taking his hand, I led him through the crowd, back

58

to my people.

Nora spotted him first. "Oh!" she yelled over the music. "Nathan!"

"Hey, sugar." He flashed her a smile while placing a hand on Riah's back. Riah turned with a grin and they sort of half embraced.

"This is Owen!" I shouted, so everyone could hear me. "Mai! And Aubrin!"

Nate slipped between Riah and Aubrin, reaching for her hand and raising it up in the air so she could do a little turn and wiggle. Making it more about him than Riah.

"Can I buy you a drink?" he asked her.

She studied him a minute, then looked back at Riah as if for permission. Riah missed it, but Nate didn't. With a scowl, he tugged her away.

A few hours later, she'd clearly had more to drink than the rest of us. Whether this was because Nate was encouraging it or because she would've anyway, it was hard to tell.

When she wrapped her arms around his neck and tried to make out with him, I stopped dancing with Nora and Mai.

Are you placing thoughts in her head? I asked.

You think I need to place thoughts to get a drunk girl to kiss me? As if to prove a point, he didn't kiss her back, instead spinning her so her back was against his front.

Now, though, Aubrin was watching Riah, and Riah, who'd been talking to Owen, was watching Aubrin.

Riah stepped over to me and whispered in my ear. "What's

happening with them?"

"Why do you care?" I asked.

"I just don't think he should take advantage of her."

"Why would you assume he's taking advantage of her? Maybe she's using him."

"Why would she be using him?"

I laughed.

"What?" he asked.

Are you serious?

"What are you laughing at me for?"

"You don't know why she'd be using him?" Could he really not see how she might be trying to make him jealous?

"I think we all know it's more likely he'd be using her," Riah said.

"Because she's such an upstanding individual that she'd never use someone?" Okay, it was probably more about what he thought of my cousin, but still.

"Are you saying she's *not* an upstanding individual?"

I gaped at him. He wasn't so naïve to believe that just because you were a wolf, you had integrity. But that sure seemed to be what he was saying. "Yes," I spat at him. "That's exactly what I'm saying."

We stared at each other as the room raged around us. Nora and Mai danced behind me, Owen chatted with some kid no one knew on our left, and Aubrin swayed in Nate's arms to our right.

They were all close enough to probably hear us shouting at each other. Everyone was close enough; it was suffocating in here.

Then again, it was also loud.

"Grace." Riah's brow furrowed and he lowered his voice. "Are you actually jealous?"

"Riah." I crossed my arms. "Are you actually blind?"

"What the hell's that supposed to mean?"

"It means she'd use him to make you jealous. And he's certainly not using her to make me jealous, I'm his cousin!"

Riah looked taken aback. "I only meant he'd use her for... for her... you know, for her body."

"Mm. Because she's got such a nice body and you noticed?"

With this, his anger crumpled—if it had even been anger in the first place—and he slid his cheek against mine. "You have no reason to be jealous," he whispered. "I'm not Christian."

And this hit me. That being cheated on once could make me lose my mind like this, two whole years later.

"I feel obligated to make sure she's safe, that's all."

"I know."

"Do you, though?" He rubbed a thumb along my jaw, eyes skirting to my lips as the party—the people, the music, the heat—swam around us. "Do you really, truly understand how I've only ever been running straight in one direction?"

"Then let me come camping," I said, before I could think better of it. It was an ongoing argument that had ruined more than a few nights.

"Grace, you know I'd give you literally anything but that."

Before I could take it back, Aubrin was slipping her way between us and attaching herself to Riah like she was an octopus—eight hands and a million suckers, her mouth kissing up his neck, heading for his face.

I stood less than a foot away, horrified, as he caught her wrists and gaped at her.

Her expression was a bit slack, sort of reminiscent of someone who wasn't exactly thinking for themself. Riah and I turned to Nate, who was snickering and, as usual, clearly pleased with himself.

Mai, Owen, and Nora were still, staring at them. Nora's eyes darted to Nate and then to me, understanding and a little bit of horror crossing her face.

Riah sharpened his gaze. "He's playing with fire." Because Owen might know what a dendrite could do, and Nate had just controlled a mind for all the world to see.

No surprise, really, as we already knew Nate liked to play with fire.

Aubrin started a PG-rated strip tease type thing, using Riah as the pole. Panicked, unable to sort through what was happening and how fast, I fogged her to make it stop. Mai and Owen too, so they wouldn't ask her later what the hell she'd been thinking. Protecting her, for Riah's sake.

Aubrin faltered, stumbling away from Riah into Nate's arms. Owen's forehead creased. Mai took it like a good, oblivious human should. As if nothing had—

"What just happened?" Aubrin asked.

To Nora, Riah said, "You got Mai?"

She nodded and he motioned Owen toward the stairs. "Come

on, Wilder." Grabbing Aubrin by the arm, he dragged her out as well. She smiled up at him, then looked back at me, then smiled up at him again.

Mai gave me a look, like she missed something, because why would Riah be leaving with Aubrin?

Yeah, good question.

I shoved through the crowd after them, and as the house spit me onto the front lawn, Riah had Owen and Aubrin on the sidewalk.

"*Dude*," Nate called from a step behind me.

Riah spun. "Did you just 'dude' me?" Leaving Owen and Aubrin, both still looking a bit dumbfounded, Riah marched up to me on the grass. "Are you perfectly okay that he just played with innocent people like they were marionettes?"

"I wouldn't say she's innocent," I replied.

"I only encouraged her to do what she wanted." Nate shrugged. "No harm in that, bro."

I glanced at my cousin. *Why, though? I didn't need to see it to know.*

He rolled his eyes to me. *To make Riah as uncomfortable as he should be, her hanging around. You're welcome.*

Riah ran a hand over his face. "I can't believe you're backing him right now. I can't believe you're okay with this behavior."

"I didn't say I was okay with it."

"You fogged them to cover it up!"

I froze. Riah froze. We locked eyes. He'd just used abnormal lingo in public. I forced myself not to look at Owen, lest it give away that I might know that he might know what exactly we were talking about.

"What did you just say?" Owen asked.

"Yeah," Nate said. "Did I hear that right?"

I cut my eyes over to my cousin, who looked thoroughly amused, then flung a slew of obscenities into his head, which only made him snicker.

Riah closed his eyes. "Okay, just one more time."

Hoping against hope Owen didn't know enough to know what it felt like, I fogged him again with a short swirl of nothingness. The consciousness behind his eyes blinked out for a moment.

"I feel like I've had too much to drink," he muttered.

"You have, man," Nate agreed. "A lot too much."

"*He*"—Riah said to me while pointing at my cousin—"is a bad influence."

"Dude. I only just got here."

"What'd I say about *dude?*"

"What are you gonna do about it?" my cousin asked with a smirk. "Punch me out?"

"No. But I refuse to get in a car with you tomorrow."

Nate snorted. "O-kay." Like this was a ridiculous punishment.

And maybe it was for him, but it wasn't for me. Because tomorrow was the full moon and we were supposed to drive back to Shady together, first thing in the morning. I'd been planning to hang out in town with my family while Riah found some wilderness to hunt.

This meant I would have to pick: Riah or Nate.

Chapter Six

Blind Trust

I forced myself not to check Riah's location until we got back to the dorms. If he wasn't waiting for me in the hall to talk about this, to make up before he went home tomorrow, then I'd allow myself a peek, just make sure he wasn't still at Aubrin's.

Our hallway was empty, so as Nora unlocked our door and Mai slipped into her room, I pulled Riah's location up on my phone. He was a block away, coming from Aubrin's, two dorms down.

Can we talk? I texted. **I don't want you to hunt mad.**

Nate wandered the room quickly once, then came back to my desk and rearranged my pictures so all the ones of him were in the best spots.

Nora grabbed her stuff for the bathroom and went to get ready for bed.

The best hunts happen when mad, Riah replied.

The kind that leave scars you mean. Because those kinds

of hunters weren't after deer and rodents. They were after things with claws and teeth.

"We were supposed to go home tomorrow," I told Nate, who was now poking through my drawers.

"Ah." He glanced in my direction before opening the one that held my underwear. "So now you have to pick between me and Riah." Fishing out my laciest pair of panties, he winked at me. "You put these on and—"

I threw a water bottle at his head. He ducked it with a laugh and it skipped off the edge of the drawer to tumble at his feet. "Be serious, Nathan."

The corner of his mouth twitched, like he was trying not to smile. "I like it when you call me Nathan. Makes me feel like I've been naughty."

"Nate," but I clipped it. "Will you drive to Shady tomorrow?"

He closed my drawer and spritzed himself with my perfume. "With you or by myself?"

"By yourself."

"No."

"No, what?"

"No, I won't drive myself to Shady tomorrow."

"Will you be here when I get back?"

"I have to work on Monday."

"Where? How far is it? When do you have to leave?"

He shrugged, then stretched out on my bed and put his hands behind his head.

I sat next to him. "Fine. Will you drive *me* to Shady tomorrow?"

"No."

"Nate."

"Say it and make it sound pretty."

"Nathan."

He chuckled. "I've missed you."

"Yeah, yeah." I crossed my legs and ran my hands over my face.

"I'm sorry, Grace," he said, voice soft and low, sincere in a way he seldom was. "I'm just not ready yet. To go back."

Propping my chin on my hand, I looked at him.

"I'm not ready to face them. To face Shady. I might never be."

Right. Fair enough. I patted my knees with a sigh. "Okay, I'm going to talk to Riah. Don't defile Nora while I'm gone."

He smiled brightly. "I pride myself on only defiling those who ask."

Before I even stood, he'd rolled over and made himself comfortable. In my twin bed.

In better news, when the elevator door opened, Riah was there. He stepped out and we walked silently down the hall to the staircase, the heavy door closing with an *oomph* behind us.

Immediately, he pulled me to him, tucking my frame against his. "You know what I can't get over?"

"What a brat I was being?"

"No. That I must be doing something wrong, if as long as I waited for you, as close as we've always been, you honestly think there's any chance I'm not all in."

Tears pricked my eyes and I looked up at the thick layer of dust on the underside of the steps above us. He'd never picked another human over me. Ever. Not even his ex-girlfriend, not even when they were still together.

"I don't think it's about Christian," I muttered. "I think it's the Were Code. That the moon—and by relation, Aubrin—has a pull on you I'll never have."

Wolves were attached to that gigantic piece of rock in a way that could not be explained and could not be avoided. Aubrin, as a stray, fell under this umbrella for him. I understood that, and it was something I admired about him—about them. But I didn't trust her not to use it to get what she wanted.

"That's so not true." Riah let go of me a little so he could hold my face in his hands. "You're who I'm calibrated to. Don't you see that? The only time the moon has any sway over you is when it's full. A few hours a month. That's it."

With a sigh, I leaned into him. "Can you just ask her not to touch you all the time?"

"She touches me all the time?"

"*All* the time, Riah."

"Of course. I'll make sure she no longer touches me."

"Yeah?"

"Yeah. Are you coming home tomorrow?"

I shook my head. "Nate won't go. Said he isn't ready."

Riah frowned. "I refuse to feel sorry for him right now. Don't make me."

"I don't feel sorry for him. He stole my bed."

"I could probably make some room in mine."

He'd managed to find a way to be comfortable with Owen again, and I had to hope tonight hadn't changed that. "Are you worried about sleeping there by yourself after tonight?"

He drew me into the kind of kiss that almost made me forget my question. "No," he said, in a whisper against my lips. Then, linking a pinky to mine, he yanked open the door to the stairwell. "I figure if Owen was going to care about what I was—if he actually even knows—it would be obvious by now."

—ee—

Nora and Nate were sleeping when I snuck into the room the next morning to grab my keys for Riah, my car being the only one we had in town. Then, by the time I got home from class, they were gone.

I'd told Owen I'd grab Nate and Nora and we could go to lunch, but there was a note on my bed: *Went for a drive around the lake.*

We were in Mai's room—door open—when they found us. Owen and Mai were on the futon arguing about whose playlist was better and trying to make me vote, song by song.

"Grace!" Nora's face was flushed with delight, her hands landing on both sides of the doorframe. "You should see Nate's car. I nearly took my clothes off just sitting in it."

I looked between them, at his shit-eating grin and her mussed hair, which was hard to muss, being so thick and straight and heavy that it polished itself shiny. "You've spent too much time

71

with my cousin," I told her. "You're cut off."

"No, I mean, the *leather*. I've never felt anything like it. So soft and buttery." She melted onto Mai's bed dramatically. "It smells, like, so good. And rides *so* smooth."

"That's me that rides smooth, baby." Nate winked at her and she pretended to swoon.

I rolled my eyes and they burst into laughter.

"Wait." I narrowed my eyes at him. "That doesn't sound like your dad's car."

He raised a brow. "You think I'd keep my dad's car?"

"Are you selling drugs?"

He grinned his wicked grin. "No."

"Are you selling yourself?"

He waggled his eyebrows at me. "More likely, but no."

"How did you afford a new car with leather interior so soft and buttery that Nora wanted to take her clothes off?"

"I'm selling them. The cars. Nice ones too." And this time his pride was natural, rather than posed.

I frowned. On the one hand, he was no doubt using his abnormal persuasive powers to not only get that kind of job at eighteen, but to convince customers to buy. On the other, he was more than surviving, and that's all I'd wanted for him after he left Shady.

"That's great, man," Owen said, giving me a look like I'd failed at life and wasn't the supportive cousin he expected me to be. "Sounds like a sweet job."

"It is." Nate sat down in Mai's desk chair. "Easy money, really, and I just have to chat with people all day."

Mmhmm. Chat with people.

Influence people's decisions with my natural persuasive powers. Same difference.

"Wanna go for a walk?" I asked him. "Catch up?"

I didn't know how long he was staying. Even though he didn't have to be back to work until Monday, there was something about the fleeting nature of him that made me feel like he could up and decide to leave at any moment. And I needed to talk to him about his dad. Apologize. He didn't seem mad at me, but he'd also only recently stopped giving me the silent treatment.

"Where we walkin'?"

"To the union."

With a nod, he stood. Once we were in the elevator, alone, he asked if Riah was still mad at him.

"Probably."

"You know, that wolf wouldn't be so into him if she didn't think she had a chance."

"She doesn't."

He shrugged. "She can smell his emotions, remember?"

"Don't be a dick, Nate."

"You saying she can't?"

"I'm saying she didn't go to an abnormal high school, so who knows what her parents taught her. Maybe she can, maybe she can't."

"You're just going to blindly trust him?"

"That's what trust is," I snapped. "Though it's a lot less blind after four years of utter devotion. Just because you have no one to trust doesn't mean you get to crap on my relationship."

His face clouded over as the elevator opened, and he worked his natural pout into a purposeful one. He even went so far as to cross his arms and make me open the door to the street for him.

After a few blocks of silence, I rolled my eyes. "You don't get to poke at me, and then cry when I poke back at you."

Wrapping an arm around me, he said, "But you're so fun to get a rise out of," while simultaneously saying in my head, *I have you to trust.*

I sighed. He was impossible. An impossible person to hate and an impossible person to love. A pendulum. *You do.* "Seriously though, where are you living and what are you doing?"

He caught me up on his fresh, new, normal life in Chicago while we walked to the union. And, as if I needed proof, he showed me pictures of his apartment and his cat—he had a *cat?*—along with a few selfies he'd taken with random girls he'd dated.

"Why Chicago?" I asked, as we sat on the steps by the lakeshore, huddling close against the wind.

I always told my dad it's where I wanted to go next. And it was the closest big city to hide in. I felt like I needed to hide. He stared out at the water, but I stared straight into my guilt. *I guess I thought, if he wanted to find me, he might look there.*

I let that sit a minute, waiting for him to tell me whether or not that had happened. When he didn't, I asked, "Do you think he's alive?"

He shrugged, then propped himself back on his elbows and stretched his legs out in front of us. I was hunched over, so if I wanted to look at him, I had to turn my head.

"I think," he said, "that those paramedics who had them in their ambulance were crap at their job."

"We should write the ambulance company a strongly-worded review."

"Not worth it." *They're already at a 1.5.*

I huffed out my amusement. "You checked?"

"I looked into them, the company, the dispatch, all of it."

"And you didn't find anything." It was a statement, not a question. *You think he's out there?*

They were an abnormal crew from Green Bay. So either he died on their watch and they covered it because that's what they do, or he managed to get away from them before they made it to the hospital.

I turned to find him watching me. "Nate, I'm so sorry."

He sat up and looked hard at me. "Don't be sorry for my sake. He was an evil man and deserved whatever he got. I don't want you holding this, do you hear me?"

Swallowing hard, I whispered, "Did it take you this long not to hate me?" *Is that why I haven't heard from you until now?*

"I never hated you. It just took me some time to figure out where I was going, what I should do... What I *wanted* to do. And yes, how I felt about it all. It took me some time to get him out of my head."

From the side, I wrapped my arms around him and settled my head on his shoulder. "I'm so glad you did."

75

We sat in silence for a minute as someone walked by.

"You still have us," I told him. "Always." *My mom desperately wants you home for Thanksgiving.*

He opened his mouth but didn't say anything. Then cleared his throat. "I'm not sure what bothers me more," he said, so very softly it sounded like a whisper on the wind. "That he might be alive and hasn't called, or that he might be dead and I don't miss him one bit."

Chapter Seven

It's Complicated

We took Nate bowling at Union South Friday evening, and I dreamt that night about smashing my uncle's head in with a bowling ball.

For the record, I did not smash my uncle's head in with a bowling ball. I slammed his face into the end of a banister.

That sounds worse than it was. I wasn't trying to slam his face into the end of a banister. It just happened to be all I had to work with when he charged at me.

The problem was, as much time as I'd spent searching the likely injuries from this online, it didn't seem like a person would very easily die from it, unless the impact had resulted in a skull fracture which might cause a hemorrhage or blood clot.

Two maybes. But it felt safer to think I'd murdered someone than that a monster was alive and free. Even if I didn't want to consider myself a killer.

Every time I had nightmares like this, I woke up shaking and sweaty, like I'd physically spent the night beating the crap out of someone. And then the horror would sink in, that in my sleep, I'd done so quite eagerly.

Nora was already up, her feet still resting in their basin, which did, if you were wondering, drain a bit during the night as it seeped into her. It was like watching a wilting plant come to life, a siren being in contact with water.

Due to how I woke up—slow and easy or quick and startled—she could tell if I'd had a nightmare or not, and this morning, she immediately pulsed a wave of charm over me. Even when I knew it was coming, it still managed to calm my nervous system. My heart slowed, my body stopped shaking, my breaths drew deeper.

"Two nights in a row," I muttered, reaching over to check my phone, to make sure my wolves were safe.

Riah's text had come in first: **reporting back sentient with only a split nail.**

Then Aster's: **three deer and hopefully not someone's cat.**

I dropped my phone onto the floor and cradled my aching head. "Nate?" He was sleeping in Nora's bed and she'd taken the futon, which she did most nights anyway. "Do you still get your nightmares?"

He peeked his head over the top bunk to look at me. "Girl, yes."

At least I didn't sleep walk like he did.

Dropping down to the floor, shirtless of course, he crawled into bed next to me. I pushed him away, which turned into a shoving match, then a slapping match, until I cried at him about how bad my head hurt.

This sent him on a mission to find me electrolytes and acetaminophen, a gallon of water, and plenty of protein for breakfast.

I didn't bother telling him it didn't have to do with nutrition, but rather the things that haunted me, because it was too good watching him play nurse.

By the time evening rolled around, Nate was acting like he'd taken care of a vomiting child for a week and thus desperately needed a 'stiff nightcap,' so Nora, Mai, Owen, and I took him to the union.

He wandered off to coerce the bartender into giving him a drink before we even found a table. Coerce because he wasn't of age, nor did he have a fake ID. Because he didn't need a fake ID. Because he was Nate. Meaning he had dendrite persuasion skills and no shame.

The Rathskeller glowed softly, the light spilling over the dark wooden arches and onto the heads and shoulders of everyone hunched over tables of fried food.

I, however, was there for the ice cream, so I left Nora, Mai, and Owen as soon as we found a table to head over to the newer side of the union for The Daily Scoop. Swinging out into the hallway, I ran into a girl whose apology sounded very familiar.

"Aubrin?" Her hair was down, shielding her face a bit, and she was wearing way more mascara than normal.

"Hi, Grace."

Back from the full moon already? What I truly wanted to ask

79

was if she'd bothered going anywhere, or if I should check the Madison paper for dead bodies.

"Yeah. Riah isn't?"

"It's his mom's birthday."

"Is that why you didn't invite me?"

"What?"

"Because he's not here. Is that why you didn't invite me?"

I stared at her. "I don't have your number." Riah was the only one who did. I guess I could've messaged her on social media, but had she really expected me to? Especially after Thursday night?

Except, I'd fogged her Thursday night. She didn't remember any of it.

"And you don't want it," she challenged.

"There's no use denying that," I admitted. *If you can smell my emotions.*

What Nate had said, about how she'd move on if she didn't think she hads any chance with Riah, was floating about in my brain like an acid rain cloud, and I tried to draw on what I'd said to him about trust.

There were plenty of people who wanted what they wanted and were convinced they could make it happen if they tried hard enough. It didn't have to be that Riah was putting out anything encouraging.

"What I can smell is that Riah's the only one who wants me around." Her gaze skirted away from me.

I put myself in her shoes for a minute, in a city where I'd found people who I thought would understand me, only to feel unwanted at nearly every turn. "I'm sorry, Aubrin. It's complicated."

Wrapping her arms around herself, she bit her lip. "It's really lonely, okay?"

"Of course it is. I get it." It was. I felt lonely sometimes—homesick maybe, or just unmoored—and one might say I, at least, was accustomed to huge transitions, seeing I'd done this change of life thing once already. On top of that, I had Riah, which was a bit like bringing home along with me.

To imagine not knowing anyone and hiding my true nature on top of that, plus juggling classes and homework in addition to the stupid stuff like laundry, not to mention the overwhelming notion that I was now in charge of myself?

She seemed to be waiting for me to say something more, but, "Honestly, Aubrin, I sort of thought you were only here for Riah."

"Because you didn't let me in, Grace, and he did."

I studied her, wondering if this was all a melodramatic play for sympathy, or a tactic to weasel her way in when I was right about her only wanting my boyfriend for herself.

"Who are you here with?" I asked.

"Some guys from my floor. They're kind of creeps to be honest."

"Let me buy you some ice cream." I led her down the hall and past the main entry of the union to the other side. It was the least I could do for fogging her. The most I could do was come clean, but I wasn't ready for that.

As we got in line, I asked, "Where'd you camp last night?"

"We only ever camp in Richland. My family has a lot of land."

A lot of land or no, she lived near enough the town center for that to be a questionable choice for an entire pack of wolves.

When she saw my look of concern, she said, "We pen ourselves in." Throwing her thumbs up, she wiggled them by way of explanation. Because once they were wolves, they wouldn't be able to get themselves out. "Hunting game on our land and roasting the carcasses right after is perfect cover. We pretty much fit right in."

As she ordered her ice cream, the inconsistency niggled my brain. How she said she was into the wilderness and camping, but she didn't actually leave her backyard.

"I thought you were into wilderness exploration?" I asked as we made our way back to the Rathskeller.

"I want to be a forest ranger someday. Live remote in the big parks, you know?" She licked the side of her cone. She definitely ate more like a human than Riah and Aster did. Likely a product of not having our grocery store or Al's. And I realized maybe I hadn't really been listening to her. Not enough to understand, anyway.

Before we made it back to the table, I stopped her. "If we're going to start over, I feel like I need to tell you what happened Thursday."

"Nothing happened when Riah walked me home, Grace. He's crazy about you."

"I know. But at the party, you kissed him."

82

"I what?"

"You kissed him." *And I fogged you. I shouldn't have. It wasn't fair. But I panicked. Owen and Mai and Nora all saw it and I didn't want them thinking you'd do something like that. They're already a little wary of how you act around him. Around us. Like he's your orbit and we're... not important.*

"I wouldn't have..." She wrinkled her forehead, obviously confused. "Why would you have protected me like that?"

"Because my cousin made you do it." *Well, not made. He gave you some drinks and encouraged you to act on your feelings and you complied. And I didn't think it was fair for everyone to judge you on something you were sort of coerced to do.*

She looked down at our feet, then over my shoulder, maybe at the booth we were headed to.

"I understand if you're mad at me," I said.

"You probably want me to be mad at you. To walk away and never look back."

I didn't say anything. That hadn't been my intent, but it would be a lie to say it didn't sound nice. *Are there any other wolf families in Richland?* I asked.

She shook her head. "I was so excited to meet you guys. Honestly, all of you. I'm just not great at this friend thing. My parents never let me get too close to anyone."

I lived normal, until high school, I told her. And it had been lonely. I was allowed to be close to my friends until I wasn't. And though we kept in touch, living near them now would probably make me feel lonelier than ever, since there was so much

I couldn't share and couldn't be in their presence. So much of what made me who I was had to do with the time I'd spent in Shady.

"Riah told me." But she didn't meet my eyes. "I probably owe you an apology, too. For how I acted."

"I told you, you weren't acting on your own."

"Before that. All of it. I did want him. I do." She met my gaze with a huff. "But I want friends more. And I'm not trying to convince someone I'm better for them. Even if maybe it's seemed like that."

We stared at each other for a bit, and my empathy won.

"Okay," I said. And I put the past behind us and led her over to our friends.

Chapter Eight

Deemed Undesirable

"Grace, have you heard from Nate?" my mom asked, setting the salad on the table.

I was home for Thanksgiving and everyone was here on time except for, you guessed it, my cousin.

Popping a few seasoned almonds into my mouth, I checked my phone and wished once again he'd let me see his location. "Nope."

"He did say he was coming?"

"Mom, this is Nate we're talking about. It wouldn't be like him to be on time." It would, on the other hand, be like him to change his mind, but no need to ruin it for her quite yet.

Justin's phone rang and he checked the number, then stepped into the hall to answer it. When he came back, he was much more somber than when he'd left.

"Nate fought the Sentinel on the way in," he said. "I need to go pick him up. They won't release him to anyone else."

"What do you mean he fought the Sentinel?" my mom asked.

"I mean he fought the Sentinel." My brother boxed with his fists a bit, and my mom put her hands on her hips.

Clara and I shrugged into our coats, and I gave my brother a look that dared him to suggest I not go with them. The ride was quiet and quick, and we soon pulled up to the Sentinel's new headquarters. The building was cold and utilitarian in every way, aside from the frosted, bubbled front doors that reminded me of a day spa more than a guard tower.

When the lady at the front desk spotted Justin, she radioed someone. He only nodded at her, and moments later Nate was being ushered out to us, blood leaking from various points on his face.

With a shake of my head, I went straight to the soda machine for ice pack purposes. The least they could have done was clean him up. We met in the center of the lobby and I handed the root beer over without a word.

He put the can up to his eye and wrapped his free arm around me.

"You better not be getting me bloody," I muttered, returning the hug.

"Missed you too, sugar pie."

I rolled my eyes. "You're lucky you're all beat up or I'd smack you."

"Eh, do it anyway. I like being tortured by woman."

The Sentinel at the counter waved a form at my brother, and as he started filling it out, I peeked over his shoulder. The sheet had all sorts of questions on it. Justin was currently filling out reason for stay, then length of stay...

"What are you doing?"

"Signing for him."

I looked to Clara. "No one did that for me."

"You weren't deemed undesirable."

Nathan cracked up at this. But was it because of the fight, or had he been flagged because he was my uncle's son? Was I wrong to talk him into coming back?

"Someone has to vouch for him," she explained. "Take responsibility for his actions while he's here."

"And what if I commit more undesirable acts?" my cousin asked, pushing his white blond hair out of his face.

"Then both you and Justin get a beating for it."

I stared at her, certain she was kidding. But she didn't seem it.

She sighed. "If it comes to that, they'll go easy on Justin, seeing he's Sentinel."

I waited until we were back in the car. "What in the actual hell?"

"Don't make a big deal about it." My brother about whined this at me. "I can't believe you told her that."

"She has a right to know what's going on," Clara said tightly. This was obviously a recycled argument.

"It's *true*?" I cried. "They'd beat one of their own for failing to keep some rando in line?"

"Look at me, sweets," Nate chimed in, "and tell me you don't think it's true."

I tried but couldn't. He was pretty messed up.

"Tell me what you did," I demanded. "You had to have started it."

He shrugged. "They asked me if I was a lousy nuthead like my pa, so I told them where to put their lousy nuthead."

"You didn't swing a crowbar at them or anything?"

"Well, I fought back. I mean, dude, you pull me out of my car and I'm gonna claw your face off best I can."

"I can't believe this. I cannot believe this." I could though. Was it that far a cry from what had happened when I'd been slapped? Or the times Nehemiah had goaded them into a fight sophomore year?

"Absolute power corrupts absolutely," Nate muttered.

"Why are you still working for them?" I asked my brother and Clara.

My brother glared at me in the rearview, and Clara answered, "You know why."

And I did. They were still working for them so the entire force wasn't shit. So that some days, coming into town could still be pleasant.

Justin parked in our driveway and turned the car off, then turned in his seat. "Listen, we're not telling Mom any more than we have to. She worries about the two of you enough as it is." His eyes settled on Nate. "Not a peep about being deemed undesirable, or the form, or what happens if you screw up again, got it?"

"Yeah, I got it." Nate pushed open his door. "Want me to tell her they started it?"

"She knows they can be pricks, and somewhat violent," my brother said as we met up on the walk. "I don't care what she hears about that. It's the rest she doesn't need to know."

Of course, Nate had great fun with the story. My grandpa made him tell it again, and again over pies, and again before they left.

I was shaking my head at him as I watched my grandparent's car head down the street.

"What?" He looked at me innocently.

"Every one of those stories was different."

"But each time I came out on top."

I snorted. "You are such a—"

"Devilishly handsome young man you wish wasn't your cousin so you could take me out back and—oh, hey ma."

Ma? I raised an eyebrow at him while my mom studied his face and knuckles. He winked at me.

"Do you need more ice?" she asked.

He shook his head. "Just one more piece of pie."

I rolled my eyes as my mom led us back into the kitchen. He'd already had three.

"Was there traffic today?" I asked Nate as we settled back at the table. There'd been traffic heading into Shady yesterday. Actual traffic. The truck stop was even busy, people in the restaurant and cars in the lot.

My mom set another piece of pecan pie in front of Nate and he nodded as he stuffed his face.

"Word's spreading that we're a hub for the New Age," my mom said.

"The New Age?" I echoed.

"An age of purists and elitists," she explained.

"But New Age makes it sound smarter than the Old Age." Which it clearly wasn't. Purists and elitists were not what any world needed.

"It's all about marketing, kid," Nate said, through a mouthful of pie.

I scoffed. "So we were instructed to keep Shady a secret at school, but the new council is calling people in from all over the country?"

"I'm sure they want to control the kind of people coming in."

"People who agree with them?"

My mom nodded. "As sentiment with residents sways back to the founding tenets, they need numbers from somewhere."

"What's the old council doing about it?"

"Hoping elections will tip the scales back in their favor."

"Can these new arrivals vote?"

"No, but they're such an irritant, people are leaving."

I stared at my mom as Nate managed to inhale the last bit of crumbs left on his plate. She stared back at me. She'd wanted to leave last year, and the year before that, and the year before that, because Shady hadn't been what she remembered. But most residents would never have even considered it three years ago. Not to mention, if you cared about it so much you didn't like what it was becoming, why wouldn't you stay and make sure it didn't turn?

I didn't want to know but I had to ask. "Are you leaving?"

She pinched her nose. "I don't know, Grace. My parents are here and they won't go. Justin and Clara too. Can I leave them in this mess?"

"No, you can't. And I won't, either."

She waved me off. "You're already gone, Grace."

"I'm not. This is my home. If there's a fight, I'm here for it." And I was eighteen now. So there was nothing she could do to stop me.

Chapter Nine

Tasty Treats

When Aster found out Madison had a free zoo—zoos being a new obsession of hers since she discovered the one in Minneapolis—she planned a weekend visit.

Zoos, she said, were like window shopping at a fancy restaurant.

It was an outdoor zoo in early December, but she didn't seem to care.

She picked up Jeremy in Shady on Friday night, and they made it to Madison on Saturday by lunch.

When they arrived, Aster wrapped her arms around me so tight I couldn't speak. Jeremy, on the other hand, sauntered in cool as a cucumber to casually shed his jacket. With a smug look on his face, he tossed his coat on my bed and crossed his arms, displaying a new tattoo that spanned the entire length of his right arm.

Aster rolled her eyes as she released me. "He won't wear sleeves anymore."

"The ink needs to breathe," he said, wrapping his arms around me.

"No, you just can't stop flaunting it."

Jeremy only smirked, but didn't deny it, as I extricated myself to study his arm. The lines were crisp and the ink was vivid, a collection of smaller images that fit into each other like puzzle pieces.

I pushed up his sleeve to see how far it went and was impressed with how naturally it seemed to cup around his shoulder.

"Did you get this done in Shady?" I asked.

"Yeah. New guy set up shop."

"It's gorgeous, Jer."

He winked at that.

"Vampires don't heal over tattoos?" I asked.

"Well, sure, pretty much instantaneously, but the ink's still in there."

"What'd it feel like?"

"Like the damn sun." He rotated his arm for me so I could see the underside better.

I studied the images, trying to find the common thread. There was a four-leaf clover and a rabbit's foot, a horse shoe, a penny, and a fat number seven. Was he going for luck? Were shooting stars lucky? "Are tortoises and nautical stars lucky?" I asked, dragging a fingertip across the ladybug nestled between them.

"Should this be making me jealous?" Riah asked from where he was settled against the windowsill. He tilted his head toward

Aster, who was inspecting Nora's posters.

"I had to cover all my bases, see. The dragonfly, red bat, tiger, and Chinese lantern are, of course, from China, and the Scarab is a good luck beetle in Egypt."

I pulled away at the beetle. It was eerily realistic. I shivered. "Why? I mean, what's it for?"

"Truckers at my place of employment think scrawny, albeit tall, young men with baby faces aren't tough. I got sick of them treating me with kid gloves." He shrugged and dropped his arm back to his side as soon as I released it. "Plus, Aster thinks it's hot."

She rolled her eyes and settled in next to Riah. "He's so full of himself."

"If you're trying to be tough, then why not a skeleton or a vampire or something?"

"A vampire, Grace? Surely you think I'm more original than that." He threw an arm around my shoulders. "And why I went for luck, well, that depends on who asks."

"What if I ask?"

"Then I say I need all the luck I can get."

"What if someone else asks?"

"Like who?"

"Like, a trucker."

"Then I say it's because I like to get lucky. And frankly, both explanations are true." He winked, and I rolled my eyes at him.

"All right." Aster clapped her hands. "Now that the ogling's over, let's go to the zoo!"

—ell—

We stopped in front of the ape habitat and Aster frowned at the sign: *Please do not stare at the apes or make loud noises. Waving your hands is also not recommended. These behaviors are taken as a threat and will upset the animals.*

"Hmm. That's super tempting."

Laughing, I pushed her past the lions before she could get any ideas about challenging them.

At the seal habitat, she rubbed her stomach. "So very many tasty treats."

"Zoos are like a very unsatisfying trip to the grocery store," Riah agreed.

"The otters are my favorite, okay?" I linked arms with Jeremy, who was the only other one here to enjoy the animals as they were, apparently, which was alive. "I'm telling you now so you don't make any unsavory remarks about them."

Jeremy stopped me in front of the giraffe's sign, and with a soft tone, read it out loud. Only, when he got to the end, he kept going: "Giraffe blood is known to relieve the pain of a snake bite. Due to the animal's strong pulse, giraffe blood can enter a vampire's system very quickly, though suction can be a bit messy. Recovery from snake without giraffe blood: four hours. Recovery from snake with giraffe blood: seven minutes."

I grinned. "Sometimes I love you."

"Sometimes I love me too."

When we moved on to the rhinoceros pen, I asked him to do it again.

"The rhinoceros is most easily slit and drunk from the belly. This animal's life water will help focus a vampire's blood to his or her groin in order to aid in the act of—"

I elbowed him in the stomach.

"I'm serious!" But he was laughing. "I swear I'm serious. I'm not just being me."

I narrowed my eyes at him.

He put up his hands in surrender, his laugh having faded to a grin. "Do you want to hear the rest or not?"

I crossed my arms, unsure. "Or not," I decided. But as we moved on to the camels, I couldn't help but ask how he knew all this.

"What do you think I learned about in school?"

"How to use animal bloods, but...the rhino?"

He smirked. "You can't keep that from horny teenagers. They'll sniff it out."

"Okay, fine. Tell me the rest."

I was grateful we were here in December, instead of high season, because that meant we hadn't seen one other person. The snack house was even closed. Not all the animals were out, but it did allow us to have this conversation.

"The buffalo is for acute bone injuries or significant muscle tears," Jeremy said, as Aster and Riah goaded the badger nearby with taunts about how they could tear its skin off from foot to limb and other nonsense like that.

You can imagine how they acted when we reached the bears.

Or maybe you can't, but Jeremy and I were still laughing about it when we met up with everyone for dinner. Though I made sure to instruct Aster and Jeremy that there would be no talk, no stories, nothing to give Owen any idea that any of us might have ever had reason to actually fight a bear or eat a badger in the wild.

Everyone was to be on their best behavior. If Nate had very nearly managed this for a weekend, then Jeremy could surely manage one night.

After all the introductions were made and the general getting-to-know-you questions asked, Mai brought the subject around to Vicious Bites.

"You into vampires?" Jeremy asked, sliding his forearms onto the table to show off his tattoos.

No, Jeremy, I told him. *Behave.*

He only winked at me. As much as Riah liked to show off, I forgot how much worse it could be.

"Who *doesn't* like vampires?" Mai asked, in all seriousness.

"Honestly, Viktor—the love interest in Vicious Bites—reminds me of you, now that I think about it," Nora told Jeremy, as if she didn't know any better.

With a smirk, he slung an arm around Aster, who was sitting next to him in the corner of the big booth. "Tell me more."

"He does have a forearm tattoo," Mai offered, eyes slipping to the ink on Jeremy's arm.

"Can he throw a mean axe?"

Looking confused for a second, Mai asked, "You can throw an

axe?"

"Sure can."

I kicked him under the table. He didn't flinch. *Can you please do something to shut him up?* I asked Aster.

"Are axes a northern Wisconsin thing?" Mai asked, as Aster turned Jeremy's face to hers, planting a kiss on his lips.

Not just any kiss, either.

When I realized this was all she could come up with to shut Jeremy up, I stifled a laugh. It definitely put a pin in the conversation.

Riah recovered first. "There are a lot of trees to throw axes at. And not much else to do."

"Does anyone else have a tattoo?" Mai asked.

All of us shook our heads, except for Owen.

Mai gaped at him. "Owen, have you been holding out on us?"

His fingers ran over and around a divot on the table. "It's stupid."

Nora grinned. "My money's on a moon tattoo."

"Or the NASA logo," Mai agreed.

"Actually," Owen stressed, looking at them both like he was amused but that they maybe didn't know him as well as they thought they did. "It's a family crest. We all get them at sixteen."

"The Vicious family has a crest!" Mai cried, bouncing in her seat. "Owen, are you a vampire?"

Jeremy and Aster stopped kissing, both of them at once.

I warned you about her vampire obsession.

Owen snorted. "For sure not. The sight of blood makes me

positively gag."

"When I think of family crests, I think of English nobility," Aster said casually, though I could sense the tension in her tone. She was trying desperately to change the subject.

"Not English nobility," Owen said. "Anyway, as much as I want to distance myself from what it represents, I try to think of it as a way to honor my brother."

"Okay, well, *show* us," Nora prodded.

Lifting up his shirt, Owen revealed a fist-sized tattoo on his ribcage. He dropped his shirt just as fast, so all we got was a quick glimpse, but a quick glimpse was all I needed.

I gripped Riah's thigh as Jeremy succumbed to a coughing fit, while Aster couldn't seem to take her eyes from the spot.

Close your mouth, I told her.

"What?" Nora asked. She was sitting next to Owen but on the opposite side. "I didn't see."

"That must have hurt," Jeremy forced out, as Aster muttered, "You're *ripped.*"

It's the Hand of Humanity emblem, I told Nora.

I mean, I hoped not, but there was no other reason we were all reacting the way we were. Riah's thigh was hard muscle beneath my hand, and the rest of him just as tight. He hadn't moved or maybe even breathed since he'd caught sight of it.

A family crest, my ass. That was the organization's logo. My mom said she'd seen it out in Chicago on occasion, stamped into curing concrete or carved on a tree. The one time I remember seeing it, in real life, was on the ring of one of the men who'd tried to smoke us out of Shady freshman year. Their end goal? To hunt us down, one by one, for sport.

Like the vicious animals they thought us to be.

"I don't feel so well." Riah pushed his burger toward the center of the table.

Thank God for Mai, who never saw a gap in a conversation that she wasn't happy to fill. She started in on the history of tattoos and family crests.

Maybe I saw it wrong, I said collectively to Riah, Aster, Nora, and Jeremy.

"I need to potty!" Aster said, too brightly. "Who's with me?"

"I am," Jeremy replied. Riah was still hard as steel and Nora was perched oddly like a mannequin. I noticed she'd laced her natural charm up, as if it might give her away to Owen, now that we knew, without a doubt, he indeed had some intel on our general makeups.

But maybe he'll sense it's gone, then, I told her. *Maybe that's worse.*

She nodded, which made it look like she was in for the bathroom too, then breathed out slowly, letting whatever peace she normally put out into the universe dissipate from her once again.

It helped ease my most alarming thought: Owen's family did not only know of our general existence but also actively hated us. Most likely, his brother had died on the job, believing we'd be the ruin of them and theirs. Of society and all that was good.

This, why his mother was so certain a vampire had killed him.

He said he wanted to distance himself from what it represented,

I said. It was all I had to hold on to.

"Grace," Aster snapped at me. "I said I needed to go potty."

"I said I was in," Jeremy said.

I stared at them and Riah prompted me, "You need to get out."

"Oh. Right." I was on the end: me, Riah, Aster, and Jeremy. Nora, Owen, and Mai opposite us.

Once we'd slipped into the other room and the bar crowd, I turned to them. "Maybe I saw it wrong."

"You certainly did not," Jeremy said.

"What are we gonna do?" Riah asked. "That's my *roommate*."

Aster spun to place her hands on his shoulders and shook him werewolf hard. "You're gonna pull it together. You're gonna act like nothing has changed."

"But it has."

"He doesn't know that. So even though everything changed for you, nothing has for him. That's where you live."

Chapter Ten

A Citizen Pass

We made it through the next week by avoiding Owen as best we could, while also not avoiding him so it wouldn't seem obvious we were avoiding him.

By that, I mean Nora didn't avoid him, and Riah slept in our room every night. As soon as I was done with class Friday, we left for Shady, because my nerves couldn't take a whole weekend of worrying about what might slip in front of a member of the brotherhood.

Nora almost didn't come with, but I was having a hard time leaving her there, alone, so she finally agreed.

All we had to do was make it through exams next week. Then we'd be in Shady for an entire month, not having to worry about how Owen belonged to the Hand of Humanity. We could regroup. We could come up with a plan.

There wasn't as much of a line to get into town as there had been over Thanksgiving, but the parking lot of the truck stop was packed. As if it were now a hangout.

When we reached the Sentinel's line, we all had our driver's licenses ready and our windows down.

"Sorry, guys." The Sentinel at Riah's door hooked his thumbs in his belt loops instead of taking his license, and no one even bothered to come to my window at all. "We're not letting anyone else in today."

"You're not what?" I asked, leaning over to see his face.

"We've met our quota. You'll have to turn around and try again tomorrow."

"But we live here," Nora said.

"If you lived here, you would've whipped out your citizen pass, not your driver's license."

"Where are we supposed to go?" Riah asked.

The guy shrugged. "Not my problem."

As Riah swung my car around to park on the other side of the road, I dialed my brother's cell.

"Yello," he answered.

"Can you come get us?" I asked.

"Um, no? I didn't know you were coming home."

"Well, we did. So come get us."

"I can't, Grace, I used up my quota on Aster and Christian."

"What quota?"

He grunted, like he was repositioning. "Listen, you can't just show up here anymore."

"What do you mean I can't just show up here anymore? I *live* here. This is my *home.*"

"Yeah, well. You're going to need to make that official."

"What the hell is that supposed to mean? And how is it my fault for not telling you ahead of time? Don't you work for these idiots?" I looked over to Riah, who was resting his head back on the seat, his eyes closed. Nora was on the edge of hers, head bent to listen in on our conversation.

"You can't assume, just because we're Sentinel, that we can always pull strings for you."

"Why not?" I grumbled. "Isn't that the point of you being Sentinel?"

"It was the point," Clara's tone replaced my brothers. She always stole the phone from him when he got snippy with me. "But our hands are a bit tied these days."

I sighed, relaxing my tone since she wasn't my stupid brother. "So what, we're just supposed to turn around and go back to school?"

"Try Jeremy," she suggested. "If nothing else, he can keep you at the truck stop for the night and you can come over first thing in the morning."

"That's ridiculous," I said.

"I'm sorry, Grace. It's the best we can do."

She hung up. End of conversation.

Riah was staring at me, dumbstruck, and I was staring at my phone.

"That's an actual no?" he asked.

"That's an actual no. Think your dad can get us in?"

He shook his head. "My dad's on the other side. That would

just piss them off."

"Clara said to see if Jeremy can keep us for the night." But as far as I knew, there were no beds at the truck stop.

Riah pulled back onto the road and drove us the short way there, parking in the first spot we saw. Piling out wordlessly, we wound past people chatting by their cars like they were tailgating at a football game. It reminded me of the vampires who congregated in town in the middle of the night when they couldn't sleep, or how the wilds had crept along our sidewalks when Samuel sent them all to Shady sophomore year.

We shoved through the front doors into the little lobby that separated the gas station from the bathrooms from the bustling diner.

Sure, it was a reasonably small restaurant, but still. It had never—in all of history, I was willing to bet—been this busy.

Instead of taking the door to my right for the diner, or the one straight ahead for the bathrooms, I slammed through the one to my left, into the gas station. Jeremy was easy to spot, head tall above the shelves, and I made my way over to him at the counter. Riah and Nora trailed behind, Nora staring wide-eyed at all the wild and not-so-wild abnormals slinking around us.

Jeremy wasn't working the register, but scratching out who-knows-what on a clipboard.

I approached the counter opposite him and put a hand on my hip.

He looked up, grinning as the recognition dropped over his face. "Hey! What are you guys doing here?"

"The stupid Sentinel won't let us go home."

"And here I thought you missed me." He held out his fist for Riah and they exchanged a modified fist bump. Then he turned his attention to the werewolf next to Nora, who was disheveled and obviously only partially tamed, based on the fact that she was poking a pen up her nose.

"That's for writing with, you imbecile, if you even know how to write," Jeremy muttered. "We don't sell anything here that you insert into a nostril."

She went to put it back but he let out a loud, "Naw. You *will* be paying for that."

"Imbecile?" Riah asked, with a raised eyebrow, as we watched her get in line.

Jeremy rolled his eyes to him. "Seriously? You think I care who I might insult?"

"Wilds are people too," Riah grumbled.

"Please don't get me started. You have no idea how much harder my life is with them roaming around."

"Jer, we can't get into Shady," I said, reminding him of the reason we were here.

"I can try and smuggle you in, but it could get us shot."

The three of us gave him varying degrees of looks.

Jeremy shrugged. "I'm not joking. It's sort of crazy around here. But hey, I can get you a table. You hungry?"

I pulled out my phone.

"Who are you calling?" Riah asked.

"Aster. I was supposed to meet her at Parrino's." Stella was working tonight, and we'd been planning on surprising her. "Maybe if we can't get in, she can at least come out."

"She can't." Jeremy took my phone and started walking. We followed him through the vestibule into the diner. "Aster would need a citizen pass to get back in, which she doesn't have. And she can only get one of those during normal business hours."

"Is that what Justin meant by making it official?"

"Probably." Jeremy nodded at any number of booths in greeting as we passed. "You really should get one."

"If we had one, would we have gotten in tonight?"

"If they were in a good mood." Jeremy slid into a booth in the back with his clipboard. It looked like an inventory sheet, which was ironic, since a few months ago I was willing to bet everything on the shelves had been sitting there for at least a decade.

Jeremy handed us each a paper menu from the holder. "Don't get the meatloaf. It's garbage."

A waitress rushed over to us. She was at least ten years older than we were, but sounded like she had a schoolgirl crush when she asked *Mr. Holmes* if he was eating.

He smiled, but it was a boss smile, short and polite, something I'd never seen on him before. "Candy, I've told you, you can call me Jeremy."

I narrowed my eyes at him. "You did not just call her candy. Have you no respect for the female sex?"

Setting his elbows on the table, Jeremy steepled his fingers to set his chin on them, then gave me an irritating smile and his full attention.

"What?" I asked.

Riah cleared his throat. I looked at him, at his head directing my eyes to her nametag, where it said, quite clearly, 'Candy.'

"I'll have you know, Grace James, that I have not even slept with this fine lady right here."

I glanced at her apologetically, that this was a conversation being had, but she didn't seem to mind.

She leaned over in my direction, as if she was telling me a secret. "Mr. Holmes won't date any of us. He's too noble for that."

I raised an eyebrow, but Jeremy was shoving Nora out of the seat next to him to launch himself in front of vampire who was charging a wolf with a steak knife. It sunk deep into Jeremy's belly but didn't faze him. He punched the vampire, pulled the knife out of his stomach, handed it to Candy, and grabbed the vampire by his long, tangled hair.

Jeremy dragged him through the restaurant, and we watched through the window as he deposited him out front. They yelled at each other for a minute and then Jeremy stalked back in. He was holding his stomach like I might, if I felt like throwing up, only the dark tinge of vampire blood was oozing out between his fingers.

He slumped down next to Nora, and Candy said she'd be right back with some raccoon.

"You just happen to have raccoon around here?"

"I have a plethora of rodents out back." He sucked the air in through his teeth. "It's not the best set up for them, but it's all I got. Dr. Riley's breeding as fast as he can, to keep me in meds."

"I take it this is all in the natural course of business these days?" Riah asked.

"The stabbing?"

Riah nodded.

Jeremy shrugged. "We might as well be living in a lawless zone. TAKE IT OUTSIDE, STEVE!"

I turned around and the wolf who'd almost been the knife victim was taunting the others who'd been sitting with the vampire Jeremy kicked out.

Steve flipped Jeremy off, but headed outside as he was told, only to immediately start throwing fists with the vampire he'd originally been arguing with inside. There were people milling everywhere, and no one bothered to do anything about it. Not even when Steve pulled the guy's throat out.

Clasping my hand over my mouth, I thought I might be sick. Doubly so, because everyone just watched as if it were a movie—*I* just watched as if it were a movie.

"Don't worry," Jeremy said gently. "I've got clean-up crews."

"What is *happening*?" I cried.

"This is how the wilds have always lived," he reminded. "It's how the purists and elitists want to live. And the council has invited that to our doorstep."

"The new council," I corrected.

"Except they're not so new anymore. Here, focus on my arm." He laid his tattooed forearm out for me, which was only slightly spattered with blood.

"You do need all the luck you can get," I whispered.

"Don't worry about me. I'm nearly indestructible. And the rest of the night should be calm. Once somebody dies, everyone's usually on their best behavior."

"Jeremy," Riah looked over to him, jaw tight. "Please tell me you're kidding."

"Does it look like I'm kidding?" he asked as Candy returned with a racoon head, freshly cut from its body to bleed into Jeremy's wound. He nodded at her as she handed it over and said, "We're ready for drinks. Hard ones."

I shook my head. "I don't want anything. I can't eat."

"I'm not talking food, Grace."

"No! I will throw up. Do you want me to throw up?"

"I don't really drink," Riah said.

"Me either," Nora added.

"You'll want to, with what I'm about to tell you." Jeremy put up four fingers and Candy slipped away.

What could he have to tell us that was worse than what we'd seen already?

He drummed his fingertips on the table for a minute, studying each of us in turn. "The old council might not have come to terms with this yet, but we're overrun. Too many have left. Even some of the wilds who just built houses out behind your house, Grace. They came for what Shady was, and they left because it's not that anymore."

Jeremy paused as Candy slid a drink for each of us onto the table. I looked up at her, wondering how many of them she had ready and waiting that she could get them to Jeremy that fast.

A boy walking by stopped hard in front of Nora, and a wicked smile spread across his face.

"No, Wilson. This is my friend. Carry on." The expression Jeremy turned on Nora was apologetic. "He only wants in your pants."

Nora swallowed hard, pulled one of the glasses of amber liquid toward her, and downed it. The first taste of alcohol that had ever passed her lips.

Jeremy grinned and put an arm around her. "You're a rock star, and I will totally take those pants if you want to give them up."

I kicked him, hard, under the table.

"*Damn*, Grace." He nursed his shin.

I kicked him again, because the bruise was probably already gone.

"All right, all right." And he pulled his arm back to himself.

"What does this all mean?" I asked. "What happens if this is the new normal and we don't do anything about it?"

"It means this kind of behavior leaks over to Green Bay, or Marinette," Riah muttered.

"Or both," Jeremy agreed, tapping his glass to the one untouched in front of Riah.

"So what, Wisconsin just turns into a wild's playground?"

"Probably not the bigger cities down south, but the Northwoods? Yeah."

"No one would be safe," I said.

"Indeed," Riah agreed.

"Particularly not your humans." And with this, Jeremy tapped my untouched glass. Back when Charlie came to Shady freshman year, Jeremy had referred to her as 'my human.'

It didn't seem so funny anymore, watching how the wilder abnormals interacted with each other. They hardly valued each other's lives, of course they wouldn't value a human's. Which meant they *were* mine. To protect.

Because if I didn't do it, I couldn't imagine who around here would.

Chapter Eleven

That's Not Who I Am

Jeremy set us up on cots in the storage room Friday night, and by the time I woke up Saturday morning, I'd decided it was time to come clean to Owen.

If his family was Hand, then they'd be the first to find out about a town gone amok. And if that happened, I wanted him to know that's not who we were.

I hoped that simply knowing us, he'd know that. But I didn't want there to be any doubt. I didn't want him to lump us in with them, if that's what it looked like we came from.

Nora was on board, but it took us all week to convince Riah. Which was fine. Better to tell Owen the truth—horrifying as it might be for him—and then leave town for a month, just in case he felt compelled to kill us. It would give him some time to digest the news, remember how much he loved us, and come around before we all headed back to school in January.

Did we really have a choice? At the rate things were devolving in Shady, Wisconsin itself might blow up.

As many reasons as I had for telling Owen, Riah had that many against. The glaring one being that we'd be putting a target on our backs. But ultimately, we were on the same side. We didn't want to kill our own kind, of course, but we did want, and had always aimed, to protect his kind from the worst of us.

That's what did it for Riah, I think, this cause I'd taken up to protect the humans, and the fact that they could so easily get caught in the crossfire of whatever was happening in Shady. If they did, then Owen should know we were pacifists. And that we were willing, perhaps ironically, to fight for a world where pacifists could still exist, and where everyone, no matter who or what they were, could thrive.

It was good that Riah finally agreed, because truth be told I might have done it whether he wanted me to or not. He said if it went poorly, he could always just drop out of school. Aubrin said if it went poorly, the two of them could sublet an apartment on the other side of campus.

So that was still the dynamic, no matter what she'd said to me that night at the Rathskeller.

This was how Riah, Nora and I found ourselves waiting for Owen to come back from his last exam on the Thursday before Christmas. Mai and Aubrin were done with finals and had already headed home for break.

Riah paced his small room, Nora was leaning against the bed-post picking at her fingernails, and I sat on Riah's desk chair, ready to do the talking.

Nora's charm was wafting casually through the room when Owen walked in, and whether it was that or the three of us sitting quietly, he stopped hard to assess us.

"Everything okay?" he asked. "Is Mai okay?"

"Yeah." I waited a beat for the charm to really settle. "We just need to talk to you about something."

"Sure." He dropped his backpack by his closet and sat in his desk chair across from me. "Have at it."

I leaned forward, elbows on my knees. "We love you, Owen. You know that, right?"

"Are you guys bailing on me for next year?"

"What?"

"Our apartment. Are you bailing on me?"

I stared at him. The four of us and Mai had signed a lease together in the beginning of the year. It was ridiculous how early students had to commit to this kind of thing, and it had been over and done so fast, I'd forgotten all about it. How this hadn't hit me at any point when finding out about him being Hand, I didn't know.

"After you hear what we have to say, you might want to bail on us," I told him.

"No way. You guys are my family."

"Okay, then." I took a deep breath in. "So, Shady Woods."

He narrowed his eyes, but his cheeks were still soft. "Yeah."

I nodded. "What do you know about it?"

The room was still. Time slowed. It wasn't Nora's charm, but us holding our breath. We'd told him we were from Marinette.

"What do *you* know about it?" he asked.

"I know..." What did I know? What was the nicest, simplest thing about Shady? If I had to distill its intended essence? "I know it's a haven."

He nodded intently, warm brown eyes in mine. "Yeah. Me too."

"Yeah?" I was wading here. Taking my sweet time. It was quite unlike me.

"Yeah." His brow furrowed. "My dad always told us to stay away from it."

"He told you to stay away from a haven?"

"How do you know about Shady, Grace?"

Now he was wondering if we were Hand or abnormal. Or maybe humans who'd stumbled onto something we didn't understand.

"We're not from Marinette, Owen."

A small smile tugged at the bottom of his lip, and he leaned back in his chair. "I know you're not from Marinette."

"What do you mean you know we're not from Marinette? We told you we were from Marinette."

He laughed a little, then wiped the amusement off his face with the back of his hand. "Yeah, and you'd never heard of Mickey Lu's. Kind of gave you away."

"What's Mickey Lu's?" Nora asked.

He glanced over at her. "Exactly." Owen's eyes skipped over Riah, then back to me. "So you're here to tell me you're from Shady Woods?"

"You... you knew?"

He shrugged. "I guessed."

"Owen." I stared at him. What did this mean? He'd guessed we were abnormals and he just let us freak out all this time? I stood up. "What the hell?"

"Grace," Riah warned.

"We know what your tattoo means! Was that fun for you? Watching us freak out?"

"Hey." He reached for my hand but I ripped it away from him. "I told you that's not who I am."

I was seething, breathing heavily as I stared down at him. What a complete and utter asshole.

"It was kinda mean," Nora said. "Can't you imagine how scared we were that you'd hate us?"

"Hate us?" My voice was high. "We thought you'd want to kill us!"

Owen ran his hand through his hair, an impish look on his face. "You're right. I'm sorry. Riah, I'm sorry. Listen, I refuse to operate on hatred. I figured you all knew me well enough to know that."

His eyes searched each of us out. Riah was hard to read, but was nodding his head like it all made sense. Or maybe like, yes, this had been the right decision. Nora was shaking her head with her arms crossed, but then she let out a short laugh.

I was… I don't know what I was.

"Grace, I don't want to be in a cell." Cells were what the Hand of Humanity called their smaller units. "I've never wanted to be in a cell."

"Why'd you show us that tattoo, if it wasn't to terrorize us?"

"Because Mai asked if I had one, and I didn't want to lie to my best friends." He looked up at me, beseechingly. "I felt like I was lying to you from the moment you fogged me at that party, same as you probably felt like you were lying to me. I didn't want that. Honestly, I hoped that maybe, since I was so outnumbered with Aster and Jeremy there, that you might tell me the truth then."

"Damn, Owen." Riah shook his head. "You've known since that first party?"

Owen grimaced. "I was well trained. Had to read, from multiple accounts, over and over again, what it felt like to be fogged or charmed."

"We've wasted a hell of a lot of time worrying about this."

He shrugged. "I showed you. You could've shown me."

"I can only show you on the full moon," Riah muttered. "And ain't nobody wants to see that." He gave me a pointed look.

I ran my hands over my face. "Do you know what a purist is? An elitist? Have you heard the term New Age, as it pertains to abnormals?"

"Purist and elitist, yes. New Age, no."

"The semantics don't matter," Riah said, stepping over to lean on his desk next to me. "Shady isn't much of a haven anymore, and though we're hoping to fight for it, to get it back, if word

120

gets out, we wanted to make sure you knew we're old Shady. Not this new thing that the purists and elitists are trying to make it. That's not what we come from. That's not who we are."

"Wait," Nora interrupted. "Does this mean you'll still live with us next year?"

Owen grinned at her. "You can't get rid of me that easily."

"Does this mean you're not going to put us on some kill list?"

Owen's lip twitched, as if this idea was amusing. "The way I see it, Grace, we're on the same side."

Riah nodded. "That's our whole point."

"I'd lay down my life to protect you, Owen," I vowed. "And Mai. Humans in general. I want you to know that."

Owen glanced at Riah. "I wouldn't have pegged the dendrite for the lead soldier."

"She tries," Riah said.

"Hey!" I cried. "I could take both of you!"

Owen's eyes twinkled. "How 'bout instead, you just let me see what your hands can do. My mom's told me stories."

But I was too busy pouting. Still, as I crossed my arms defiantly, I let the sparks fly.

Chapter Twelve

This is Not Okay

Aubrin showed up on my porch a week after New Years.

"You shared your location with me!" she explained.

This was true. She'd badgered me until I caved, which happened at some point during exams when I was overworked, exhausted, and sleep-deprived.

"Is this *why* you wanted my location?" I asked. "Don't you have Riah's?"

"Not after you told him I couldn't touch him," she said cheerily, bouncing into my foyer and looking around. "I have to hand it to you. Aside from the big dudes blocking the road on the way in, this town is *adorable*."

"Did Riah tell you that? That I told him you couldn't touch him?"

"Of course not, but I inferred." She wandered left into the kitchen, then back across the entry to the living room on the right. "One day he was comfortable with it, and the next he wasn't." Down the hall to peek out into the backyard, then up the stairs.

I followed. Because I guess she was staying? And better here than Riah's. Or maybe not. Maybe I should hand him over to his sisters.

"I'm not sure it's completely safe for you to be here," I told her. "Things are kind of contentious in town right now."

She waved a hand of it. "Which is your room?"

"Straight ahead."

Dumping her bag on my bed, she spun to take in the little pieces of me that I'd left behind or grown out of, taking special interest in the axe Jeremy had carved for me that was too beautiful to leave exposed to the elements on our forest rack.

She poked through my running shoes, fingered my Parrino's nametag, smelled every one of my candles, and paged through the books on my bookshelf.

I wanted to ask her why she was here. Would that be rude?

"My parents got word Shady existed," she said, flopping on my bed and tapping her nose, implying she smelled the curiosity on me. "They wanted to make the trip with the whole family, but I told them they'd embarrass me. Really, I didn't want to overwhelm you. And I know what you said about the temperature here, so I didn't want my little brother in the middle of it."

"*You* should maybe not be in the middle of it," I countered.

She lifted one shoulder. "I like to believe I'm pretty tough, being a wolf and all. Figured it was a good test."

"Aubrin, I think..." There was no nice way to say it, so I just spit it out, "I think you've been pretty sheltered."

She nodded. "I know, Grace. And that's why I'm here. I'm trying to be more like you."

I stared at her, not quite understanding what she meant. A blush crept up her face, and she hopped up, bounding past me and heading down the stairs. "Will you teach me how to throw an axe?"

—ell—

Aubrin was downright terrible at throwing an axe.

I know because I sent Jeremy a video and asked if I'd ever been that bad, back when I first started. He replied with his own video of him just laughing and telling her not to kill anyone while she was at it.

Then she wanted to see town, all the little bits that Richland Center, where she was from, wouldn't have. Since we'd gone to Riah's for the axe-throwing, he was with us, and his sister Ava too. Maribel, the third triplet, wasn't as enamored with a werewolf who lived normal, seeing as she was a vampire, but Ava couldn't stop asking questions.

Riah was a little put out. "I live normal now too, you know. You could ask me."

We tried to get ahold of Nora, but she was likely in Iara, and there was no reception in the lake.

We took Aubrin to the cooler where she loaded up on all the meats she'd never had before, and then we stopped at the General

Store and its alley window. She thought that was the coolest thing—*climbing through a window! Down a dark alley!*—and next was the pharmacy. Apparently, there was a secret attic above it that sold abnormal products same as the window and the cooler.

"You know, I've never actually been here before," I said, as Riah led us inside the building.

At the back of the store, a little hall with bathrooms ran off to the right. The drinking fountain, which my friends called a bubbler, had a little stool in front of it for children who couldn't reach. Riah took the top step in order to rap on the ceiling.

He stepped back down and we waited a moment, long enough that I became doubtful there even was an attic up there, until finally we heard a tap, tap, tap in response.

Pushing into the men's bathroom, he held the door open for us. Ava swept right in and Aubrin looked at me. "I guess they can't very well use the ladies' room, right? What with how often we use it?"

I made a face and followed her in past the urinals. Ava knocked once, hard, on the wall by the light switch, and with that a square in the ceiling opened and a ladder was lowered down.

We scrambled up: Ava, Riah, Aubrin, and me. I was helped to standing by a strong hand, and then I saw his face.

"Nehemiah, hey!"

But he was staring at Aubrin, who was staring at him.

"Miah, Aubrin. Aubrin, Miah," I introduced them.

"You're a wolf," she said, coy.

"As are you. How come I've never seen you before?"

"I don't live here."

"Oh, I'd know if you lived here."

Rolling my eyes, I left them to flirt while I checked out this attic. Wooden beams supported the roof, and plywood was nailed down for the floor. A few short rows of shelving were sparsely populated with tubes and jars and packages. I trailed my finger along them, past the animal salves for various injuries a vampire might incur, pills that claimed to ease vampire indigestion 'from ingesting non-drinkables,' siren tear infused gingko biloba for boosting mental capacity, the list went on.

It seemed everything they sold downstairs was also sold up here, only with the added boost of vampire blood or siren tears.

By the time I swung back around to the front of the space, where the ladder and counter were, Aubrin and Nehemiah were exchanging numbers and socials.

"Will you take a selfie with me?" she asked. "So I can put our cute picture in by your name to help me remember who you are?"

"Absolutely. I'd love a selfie with you. Not that I'll need any help remembering who you are."

Riah gave me a look.

He's always been a bit forward, I told him. *Honestly, I like this for them.*

After they took one together, Aubrin slid her coat off her shoulders, adjusted her shirt so her tattooed shoulder was exposed, then grabbed his phone to take a shot of herself kissing the camera. Handing the phone back to him, she said, "I wouldn't want to risk it."

Nehemiah grinned. "You really live normal?"

"If you don't believe me, you'll have to come see sometime."

He nodded like an idiot as Ava made her way back down the stairs. Then Riah.

"Ready?" I asked Aubrin.

"Not really." But she moved toward me and the hole in the floor.

As she slipped down the ladder, Nehemiah whispered, "Holy crap, she's hot. Where you been keeping her?"

We brought Aubrin to Parrino's to show her the cellar and a bit of the tunnels, then met Stella and Ethan at Al's when it was time to eat, because Al's was where you could find the largest selection of raw meats.

As if Nehemiah and Aubrin had already shared their locations with each other, he showed up about five minutes after us. I mentioned how I didn't approve of how fast this was moving, but she promised she saved location sharing for day three.

Al was Nehemiah's dad, so it made some sense. Come to find out he'd been working at both the pharmacy and filling in at the restaurant. He was supposed to work the dinner shift but ended up sitting with us instead.

It was the first time that day I felt like maybe Aubrin shouldn't be in Shady. I know I'd said as much when she'd first shown up, but there'd been no crowds and no shenanigans until we hit Al's. Maybe because of the menu, or because it was one of the first buildings when you entered town, it had a similar vibe to the truck stop. Even though it was January, people overflowed to mill outside on the patio. Sure, it was a mild day, the sun was out, and Al's had tall space heaters on his patio, but what it said to me was that these were wilds, or they wouldn't be so comfortable with the weather and they'd just go somewhere else.

Riah must have scented my wariness, because he tucked me tighter into his side as a rowdier group walked in the front door.

Stella tracked them across the restaurant. "My dad's thinking about selling the houses."

"Houses, plural?" Aubrin echoed.

I gave her a quick rundown on how Iara worked—a home underwater linked to a home on the lake.

Stella sighed. "It's particularly beautiful right now, with the lake frozen over."

"Sounds cold," Aubrin said.

"Our body temp adjusts to whatever moisture we're in contact with. Feels no different to a siren than any other time of the year."

"Where would he go?" I asked.

"The Galapagos or Antarctica."

"Stella..."

She waved her hand as if to dismiss it. "Don't worry. I'm not going anywhere. I'd move in with Ethan probably. Winters would be hard, not having access to the water, but I could always

129

set up an ice shanty."

I glanced at Riah. "Maybe it's not a bad idea."

He raised an eyebrow. "An ice shanty?"

I made a face at him. "Is this salvageable, honestly? If citizens are leaving and elitists streaming in, our time is running out. Maybe Jeremy's right. Maybe we don't have the numbers."

"Is that Jenny Jones?" Stella whispered, her eyes on a tall, willowy woman walking in the door on Jeremy's arm. Jenny Jones was a movie star who we'd suspected of having been turned into a vampire a few years ago.

"Is it?" Aubrin asked, eyes wide. "I think it is! What's she doing here?"

Jeremy walked the woman and her companion to the counter, introduced her to Al, then caught sight of us and sauntered over. He pulled an empty chair from the table next to us and sat down.

"Ladies and gents," he greeted. Then, "Oh, hey Aubrin," and a raised eyebrow for Nehemiah, who would not normally be found sitting with us.

"Is that Jenny Jones?" Stella hissed.

"Yeah. She walked into the truck stop all confused about how to get to this place Samuel told her about, way back before he disappeared."

"Is she elitist?" I asked him.

"She's *abnormal*?" Aubrin squealed.

"Grace, I don't know," Jeremy said, exasperated. "We didn't discuss our politics."

To Aubrin's question, Stella explained the whole sordid story of Samuel and our junior year, which was, in this case, Jenny Jones' abnormal origin story.

Ethan opened his mouth to say something, but before he could, the window behind him smashed into pieces and an axe landed in the top of his skull.

Jenny Jones screamed like she'd been trained for horror films—which she had—and Stella stood up to yell out the window at whoever had thrown it, about how irresponsible they were being, throwing axes around like basketballs.

I couldn't take my eyes off Ethan, though I wanted to gape at Stella at how calm she was. Okay, so she wasn't calm, but she hadn't bothered to check if Ethan was okay with the *axe lodged in the back of his head,* rather immediately standing up to scold whoever did it and arguably putting herself at risk as well.

"Sit down!" I cried, tucking myself into the booth in case another one came flying.

Jeremy stood up, pulled the axe out of Ethan's head, then headed for the door. Nehemiah moved to back him up, being it was his dad's establishment and all, but one glance at Aubrin seemed to have him conflicted. She was wide-eyed and pressed back against the booth like a fly on a windshield. As loud as Jenny Jones was in her terror, she was silent, shaking her head and mouthing "no, no, no, no, no," on repeat.

Riah put a hand up. "I'll go." Then headed out after Jeremy.

Ethan reached up to feel under the flap of skin the weapon had created, and I nearly gagged.

"It didn't go through," he reported, replacing the loose skin and patting it into place with only a slight wince.

I gaped at him. "It didn't go through your *what*?" Because it had definitely gone through something.

"My skull, Grace. It didn't go through my skull."

"*And what if it had been someone else, Ethan?*" I cried. Anyone else. Anyone but a vampire. What if it had been Aubrin? Shady was supposed to protect us.

Al came out of the kitchen where he'd retreated with the shattering of his window, hopefully to call the cops, and charged out the front door. I stood to do the same.

Ethan held me back with the hand of his that had been *inside his head*, which left an eggplant-colored handprint on my sleeve. "It's nothing."

I stared at him, incredulous. Stella was busy crying into his ripped open head in order to heal it, and it was nothing? I shook him loose and slammed through the door to see what was going on.

Al was standing guard at the door and Jeremy was at the curb, the axe hanging loosely from his hand as it rested in the grass, tip darkened with the deep purple hue of vampire blood. Riah was a few paces behind him, arms crossed. I glanced back inside the restaurant, where people seemed in a hurry to finish their food, but not in a hurry enough to abandon their meals for sake of vacating the premises.

It had been one thing to see chaos at the truck stop—outside of town—but another altogether to see it right here on the streets that were supposed to be safe and normal. Or, as normal as they could be with a bunch of us running around.

The argument had turned into a fistfight between, as best I could tell, a wild-looking vampire and a townie. The wild had nearly beaten the other man to a bloody indistinguishable pulp, and no one was interceding on his behalf.

"Don't even think about it." Riah grabbed me around the waist as I moved to walk past him.

"Think about what?"

"Getting involved."

"I'm not that stupid."

"Maybe not, but the thought crossed your mind just the same."

"Then you do something." I looked at him, kind of surprised he hadn't already jumped in.

"I'm here if Jeremy needs me." He nodded his head and my eyes returned to the mess on the street.

For whatever reason, Jeremy deemed that moment to be the one where stepping in became necessary. He stood between them, back to the townie slumped on the ground, and stared the wild down.

Thwarted, the wild rocked on his feet a bit, then prepped to lunge at him. I could see it because Jeremy had trained me to see it. And as he saw it, same as I did, Jeremy met him with the axe, aiming it down on the soft skin that met head and shoulder.

It settled, same as it had in Ethan's head, just enough to hurt but not enough to do much damage. On a vampire, anyway.

"Are you wanting this back?" Jeremy asked, hands still on the axe's handle. "Would you like me to try for another swing?"

The wild grunted and dipped out from under it. Cars passed without slowing.

A cop rolled up to the curb, and Ethan's uncle got out, nodding at Jeremy as if to release him. The wild did get cuffed, so there was that, but everyone seemed weary more than surprised.

And just like that, it was business as usual. Stella was still nursing Ethan's head with her tears, and Aubrin was sniffling into Nehemiah's chest.

As I slid back into the seat next to her, she turned to me, shaking. "I'm taking you all home with me. This is *not* okay."

Chapter Thirteen

Shot, or Eaten?

When Aubrin said she lived on compound, she meant she lived on a compound.

At the end of the long driveway was a huge metal building, which ended up being, essentially, a parking garage. A tall metal fence that you couldn't see over and you couldn't see through extended from both sides. The front two-thirds of the building housed about thirty trucks and SUVs, while the back third held a spattering of UTVs and snowmobiles.

"You have to drive a UTV to your house every day?" Nehemiah asked.

He and Aubrin had been inseparable since the incident at Al's, which had been two days ago. It took us a bit to convince our parents and get word to Nora in Iara, in case she wanted to come with, which she did, so now the five of us were flying over rolling hills and through the snow in a UTV.

"It's all UTV trails inside. We *could* pave or gravel, but it's not as pleasant for hunting."

He motioned to the fence. "How do the animals get in?"

"There are about ten spots with sliding doors that only close on the full moon."

"What if a person wanders through?" Riah asked.

"We own acres in every direction beyond the fence and there are signs up everywhere: No trespassing or you will be shot."

"Shot, or eaten?"

She shrugged. "At that point, does it really matter how you go? We've never had any trouble. My brothers and cousins are well known for their guns and their willingness to use them. There aren't really any strangers wandering out here. Everyone knows us."

Aubrin flew over a little hill and the UTV rocked, causing Nora to grab onto me in addition to the bar above her head. There were so many little off-shoots of the trail, and additional snowmobile tracks in the snow, that I had no idea how to orient myself. We'd be screwed if we needed to get out on our own.

After ducking into a particularly thick grove of trees, we came out in a small clearing that held a modest ranch home. A couple snowmobiles were parked haphazardly in the front yard, and Aubrin pulled to a stop next to them.

She turned to Nehemiah. "Be careful around my brothers. They're very protective. I'm telling them you saved my life to start you off on their good side, okay?"

Riah snorted. "Is there no other way?"

She side-eyed him. "Not really."

Hopping out, Aubrin hurried over to Nehemiah's side of the UTV and offered him a hand.

"Okay, they're cute," Nora said. "And she's much more pleasant when cooing over him instead of Riah."

The front door opened and five men shoved their way over the threshold in the same way a pile of boys might when itching to get outside. Once out, they lined up to greet us. Or present themselves. Or block our way. It was hard to tell.

"Who's that?" the tallest one asked.

Aubrin stepped between them and Nehemiah. "Boys, this is Nora, Grace, Riah, and Nehemiah. Nehemiah, I'll have you know, caught an axe that was about to land in my very skull. He literally *saved my life*, okay?"

I could almost see their brains working, assessing and categorizing Nehemiah, deciding he was okay for now. Then, nearly as one unit, they moved their attention to Nora. After what I imagined was an awkward moment for her, she lifted a hand and waved at them.

"These are my brothers, Alex, Andrew, Aaron, Adam, and Archie."

"You all... live here?" I asked. Because not only did most of them look older than us, the house was not big enough for all these men.

The widest shook his head. "Just Archie. The rest of us have our own places nearby. But we saw a boy in Aubrin's car when you came through town."

I raised an eyebrow. "You have cameras in town?"

"We have cameras everywhere," Aubrin replied. "Helps us keep the town safe."

"From us," Archie added, proudly.

A woman peeked her head out the door. "Aubrin! Your other guests are already here!"

———ell———

Her other guests were Owen and Mai.

Mai.

Owen had told Mai. A *human*.

She bounced over to us as soon as we stepped in the house, her smile bursting. "Holy bananas, you guys! All this time and you're my absolute *heroes,* I can't believe you've been holding out on me! When Owen told me I about lost my mind. In a good way! I mean, I didn't believe him at first, of course, but then he showed me his parent's basement, which was totally creepy, I'm not gonna lie, but why would you have weapons with garlic if vampires didn't actually exist?"

I thought she'd stopped to catch her breath, but instead she let out a little scream, as if she'd just been personally introduced to a boy band.

Aubrin's brothers, who'd formed a circle around Nehemiah and Aubrin, stopped chattering to look over at her, and Aubrin's dad looked up from where he was starting a fire. Her mom peeked a head in from what I assumed was the kitchen, since she'd asked us if she could get us drinks: hot cocoa, cider, tea, coffee, wine, or maybe something spiked?

My heart was fluttering and I wondered if this was what a panic attack felt like. It hadn't been us who'd told her, but we'd told Owen, and rule number one was—

"We're not to tell the humans!" Nora hissed.

Owen sent her a soft smile. "I'm a human, Nora. You told me, remember?"

I felt like we'd done something terribly wrong. It hadn't seemed like we were breaking the rule when we told Owen, because he knew about us. But now...

Nora turned to me. "Is this why we're not supposed to tell the humans? Because they have loose lips?"

"I think we assumed you'd have a code, Owen." My stomach hurt like I'd just broke the law. Honestly, it hurt as badly as when I relived killing my uncle. "Protect the humans, you know? That's what our code is for, and that's your whole point. Keeping it all in the dark is the first step to both of those things."

"You trusted me, and I trusted her," Owen replied. "I wasn't going to cut her out. She'd have been the only one of us who didn't know what was going on."

"Nothing's going on," Riah said.

Owen motioned around the room. "This is going on."

Mai tossed him smile, then sidled up next to Nora. "Show me what you can do?" It was the kind of slink you'd pair with batting your eyelashes and asking a guy to show you his muscles, right before you swooned. "Aubrin's brothers have spent the last hour showing me what wolves can do. They can smell emotions! That

139

is *not* in the Finger Paws series."

"We can also smell illnesses and relationships," Riah added, his tone tart because he still hadn't gotten over the title of her second favorite book series.

Mai's eyes widened and she looked for a moment like she might faint.

"He can smell damn near everything," Nora confirmed.

"What can mermaids do?"

"Sirens," Nora bristled. "Did he tell you I was a mermaid?" She cut a look over to Owen and I nearly laughed. I'd never seen her so irritable. It helped ease my stomach.

Setting a hand on her arm, I sent a short burst of warmth into her psyche, warmth I drew on from the general mood of the house. Aubrin's dad stood proudly in front of the hearth where his fire was crackling, and her mom pushed through her sons to draw Nehemiah out and make him comfortable with food and drink and "sit here on this chair, it's the coziest."

Then I answered Mai for Nora, directly in her head and in everyone else's: *She can soothe people with her charm, and her tears fix all sorts of things. Honestly, they could probably transform modern medicine.*

Mai gaped at me, her shoulders sagging like her brain was melting from within.

"Can't beat being a siren," I added. "They never have to shave; the only hair they grow is on their head."

"No!" Mai cried. "Do it in my head again. *Only ever speak in my head.*"

With a grin, I brought up a memory from back home, a random lunch hour in high school, and sent it to them all. An image and feeling of safety and rightness. Friends, family, serenity. Something to fight for.

Mai let out a squeak and flung herself back onto the couch, where she'd been sitting when we walked in. Throwing an arm over her forehead, she exclaimed, "A vampire!"

"You've met one in real life," I told her. "Remember Jeremy?"

Her eyelids fluttered closed and I couldn't help but laugh.

"Okay," Owen muttered. "Don't make me regret telling you."

"Owen, it's just *brilliant.* They're brilliant."

"The problem, Mai, is that they aren't all so brilliant. Some are vicious and have no respect for life."

"You're not wrong," Riah said.

I crouched down in front of her. "Mai, you cannot tell a soul. Not your parents, not your friends, not—"

"Are you kidding? Why would I go back to my old friends when I could be a part of this? They'd never believe me anyway."

"Aubrin says you all are having some trouble up north?" her dad asked, his voice gravelly.

Riah nodded. "That's correct, sir. It's not what it used to be."

"Tell me what it used to be."

Owen listened intently as Riah described what Shady had been to him growing up, but his attention waned when their conversation turned to abnormal politics and philosophy.

"When did Aubrin invite you?" I asked him, wondering if this had been her plan, even before Shady Woods scared her off.

"I smell your distrust, Grace," Aubrin said, sidling up next to me. "I knew you'd told him, and I knew you were worried about what was happening in Shady. I wanted to see it for myself so I could back you, but when I showed up... Well, I figured it would help for Owen to see something good. And the good is here right now. Not there. You might as well be living in a war zone."

"Okay, that's dramatic," Nora said.

"You weren't even there," Aubrin countered. "I'm sure underwater, where only sirens can go, is a whole different world."

"Not untrue," I agreed.

Mai shot up to a rigid sitting position. "Wait. You, like, live *under* water? In this weather?"

"As much as I can," Nora told her.

"Have you ever known anyone with a chronic illness?" Aubrin asked.

We all shook our heads. Abnormals didn't really have chronic illnesses, but also, what a completely random question.

"We don't let ourselves get very close to humans, but I had a teacher once... Anyway, when you have a chronic illness, you don't think you're that sick because it's a little here and a little there. Every day wears you down a little more, and every day you forget what it was really like before. Until you honestly can't remember, and you don't see yourself as terribly sick. But everyone else looks at you, and they're like, holy cats, you're the walking dead."

She waited for some sort of confirmation, but Owen and Mai were the only ones nodding.

"That's you. Your town is chronically ill."

"Great, Aubrin, but I care too much to just walk away from it."

"Then build something like this. That's why you're here. To see how it can be done."

"But don't you get it? This is what Shady used to be. And the people who'd want to do this make up a whole town. Are you suggesting we move a whole town?"

"The only other option is to fight for it," her dad said, having turned from the fireplace. He and Riah were listening to us now, each of them with a hand on the mantle.

"Do you have enough people to fight for it?" her mom asked, a tray of hot cocoa in her hands, mugs complete with marshmallows and candy canes.

"No," Nehemiah said resolutely. "We don't. We might've a few months ago, but not anymore."

Aubrin looked up at him with all the adoration she used to bestow on Riah. "Then maybe we can help."

"You said it's like a war zone?" Owen asked.

Aubrin nodded.

"Then maybe we can help too."

Chapter Fourteen

Tough to Explain

We spent a few days roaming their land, poking around downtown Richland Center, and meeting every one of Aubrin's relatives until they all ran together.

Her brothers taught us how to shoot, and we taught them how to throw an axe. Nehemiah and Aubrin slipped off by themselves more and more frequently, and Mai could hardly contain herself—that she was there, that we existed, and that she was doing the same things we did.

Riah, Nora, and I took Mai back to Rochester while Nehemiah stayed with Aubrin, and Owen went to talk to his parents about helping us.

He hadn't told them we were abnormal, so were beyond anxious about how it would go. It was one thing to tell Owen, someone we knew and trusted, but it was another to tell the high general of the Wisconsin cells.

I was holding onto the fact that Owen's dad had told him

Shady was a haven; that he'd put out word it wasn't to be messed with.

Back in Madison, I poured over the high school texts Aubrin had grabbed from my room to show her brothers before we left Shady, and Nora bounced ideas off Mai as to what parts of abnormal life felt most important and beneficial to the world as a whole. We were expecting to have to prove ourselves to Owen's dad before he'd truly agree to help us. Prove our humanity, and all the reasons we were worth saving.

When I was done with my abnormal history textbook, Mai read it front to back while Riah, Nora, and I finalized our list of everything we could offer the world, if only they'd let us. Nora also made notes about the persecution sirens had endured, in case we needed to reference how humans weren't the only ones preyed upon, and how they, in fact, had a long history of predatory behavior as well.

A few weeks into second semester, the knock we'd been waiting for came. Even though we'd been expecting it, we all froze. Nora sent us a dose of charm, and as it hit, Riah tried to bat it off.

"That will not help me focus, Nora. I need to have my wits about me."

"You always have your wits about you," Nora replied, moving toward the door but only to look at it, not to open it.

"Do I look like I have them now?" he asked in a mutter, almost as if to himself.

She turned to study him. "What exactly is a wit supposed to

look like?"

Another knock, and just like that, my hands were sweaty.

I stood in front of my desk, trying to look casual, Riah leaned against my dresser, and Nora opened the door.

Owen stepped in first, then Mai, Aubrin, and Mr. Wilder, who was bulky with a marine haircut and a pit bull jaw. His eyes were not kind and his smile not easy. I forced myself to shake his hand anyway.

"Nice to meet you." The introductions went around as Mrs. Wilder also filed in and shut the door behind her.

Were we afraid they'd try to kill us all right there?

Not really. It would be too tough to explain.

Also, Riah and Aubrin were strong enough to subdue any human, and we had the powers of thought placement and charm on our side. Coercion, on both counts, if you will.

Just because two different cells, at one time or another, had tried to kill me and my family, didn't mean this third one would.

Right?

Owen's mother being there helped. Not that she wasn't brotherhood as well, but she was a breath of cool, fresh air in an otherwise stuffy room. She smelled as sweet as she looked, and was as refined as her husband was raw.

"I can't believe it's taken us this long to meet you all," she said, making up for the lack of happy her husband seemed incapable of mustering. "I've heard so much about you. Honestly, it's always the strangest things that force our hand, isn't it?"

"Heard so much about who?" Mr. Wilder grunted. "I haven't

heard a thing."

She patted him on his arm and her warm smile loosened a knot in my chest.

"You must be the siren?" she asked Nora. "Your skin is absolutely impeccable, and glowing."

"Thank you," Nora oozed. "I could bottle you up some tears—they're amazing for health and vitality."

"That won't be necessary," Mr. Wilder said.

"Would you like to sit?" I asked, motioning to our desk chairs and futon. Mai bounced onto my bed like she was about to watch her favorite movie, and the rest of us stayed standing.

Owen was tense.

Riah was tense.

Mr. Wilder was grumpy, at best.

Mrs. Wilder, pleasant.

Nora and I, wary.

Aubrin, antsy. And she kept checking her phone. It was her new normal, due to constant communication with Nehemiah who still hadn't gone back to Shady but was working with her brothers.

"Is this going to be a presentation?" Mr. Wilder asked.

"If you'd like?" I winced at how uncertain I sounded. Digging deep for half a serving of my normal confidence, I adjusted my tone and repeated myself, "If you'd like."

Owen's parents got situated next to each other on the futon, then looked up at us, expectant. I glanced at Riah, who raised an eyebrow at me, and I nodded. He nodded back, then turned to them and started in on the founding tenets of Shady Woods, how it came to be, and what the old council prided itself on. In other words, why they should help us get them back to full power.

Nora then walked them through my abnormal history textbook, pointing out all the ways we *weren't* vicious. I punctuated this by sharing little video reels from my memory. I asked if I could do so first, of course, and originally Mr. Wilder wanted me to stay the you-know-what out of his head. But after a few *oohs* and *ahs* from Mai and his wife, he must have felt left out, because he invited me in.

To summarize, Nora swiped a tear from her eye and placed it along a cut Owen had been picking at on his hand. It was small, but he hadn't let the scab be, and before our eyes it healed back to healthy skin.

Aubrin then talked about her experience growing up, and how a place like Shady only offered more of that, but away from humans completely, which the brotherhood, she stressed, should appreciate. She finished with the argument that Shady allowed a safe place for every species, and even indirectly humans, because it offered an option for those abnormals who might have tried life in the normal world but couldn't figure it out the same way she and her family had.

I concluded by painting a picture of what Wisconsin—or the world—might be like if what was happening in Shady right now did, indeed, spill out over its borders and spread. What kind of threat that could be to humans and the status quo as we all knew it.

Mr. Wilder grunted. His wife turned to him. "It does seem that their desires align with brotherhood interests."

"It *seems* that way, yes. But that's the issue, isn't it?" He crossed his arms. "They can make things seem a lot of ways to benefit themselves."

"Dad." Owen narrowed his eyes. "You think they'd lure us there just to kill us?"

"You've always been naïve, son."

"Right, right." Owen crossed his arms, a perfect mirror of his father. But with floppy hair. "Can't even live up to Todd's shadow."

Todd?

Todd.

I choked. Turned it into a cough. Grabbed for my water and chugged it.

Just hold yourself still, I commanded Riah and Nora. Riah, mostly. Nora might not know or remember that Todd was the name of the guy who'd burned Shady Woods our freshman year. If she didn't, she wouldn't be putting together that Owen's dead brother was likely one and the same. Riah, however, he knew.

The positive of this was that Todd wasn't dead, which meant Owen's brother wasn't dead. Not that we could tell them that.

The Hand of Humanity was known to be as quiet and subversive as we were, which meant their groups of three to five didn't often communicate with each other. It would make sense that Todd's cell hadn't told anyone what they were doing—arson was criminal activity, after all—but what if Mr. Wilder knew that's where Todd had last been?

Owen had described the role of the high general at Aubrin's, had said his father was the central gathering point for information, coordinating as needed, and sometimes giving orders. What if he'd never told anyone to stay away from Shady? Or what if he had, but they knew Todd had died there, and they were waiting for their revenge? What if we were walking into a trap?

My mouth went chalky. I took another drag of water, thinking I just might retch all over our floor. Riah reached for my hand, his grip possibly crushing a few bones that Nora would have to fix later.

I'd sat across Todd in a booth at the truck stop, and now that his name had pulled up that image in my brain, I could see the resemblance.

The Wilders had all retreated into themselves, lost maybe in different versions of sorrow, and Nora, Riah, and I had also gone quiet.

Mai studied us all, then took over. "This Alpha Court is quite noble," she said. "Not like bad guys at all. Listen, Mr. Wilder." And she read:

On the day the first werewolf was born, a piece of the moon broke off and fell from the sky. It nestled itself into the rocks and waited a century for a true alpha to claim it.

The first werewolf to come across it was afraid of the control it might hold over her and her kind, immediately swallowing it in the hopes it would disappear forever. As her motivation was fear, it got stuck in her throat and killed her.

The pack to find her noticed the huge lump and ripped her throat out to find the source of her death. But faced with the moon rock, a decision had to be made. They could do nothing and all turn in broad daylight, wreaking havoc on the nearby town, or they could swallow it as she had, containing its power once again in death.

Having no time to discuss this, one amongst them made the quick decision to give himself up. To swallow the stone for the sake of the others and whatever innocents might be thusly harmed.

However, as his motivations were to serve the greater good, as he was willing to give himself up for his pack, the rock slid down his throat and settled in his chest, marking him a true alpha. He didn't die, and in fact seemed unaffected. The pack didn't know what to make of this until one grew inconsolable with jealousy. The alpha, angered at the immaturity shown, phased into a great wolf, a greater one than they'd seen from him moon to moon in the past. He bared his teeth and readied to fight but didn't lose his mind or fall to the frenzy. He, the first werewolf to have perfect control.

A heavy silence settled over the room, until Riah said, "The start of the Alpha Court."

Owen's dad looked at him. "I might need to see it myself, Shady."

"You can't," Riah said. "They'll know you're a human from a mile away, and that's just not safe right now."

I sent them all a few snippets of what life was like, how the wilds, elitists, and purists had taken over.

"That's why we need you," Nora said sadly, once I'd finished.

"Doesn't look like there's much to save," Mr. Wilder said.

"What if…" My brain scrambled for something else to show him, another way for him to see us in action, aside from Aubrin's compound, which, if you weren't a fangirl but instead wary of wolf power, I imagined would be rather intimidating. Not to mention the fence and security. Like walking into a prison. "What if you came on the next full moon hunt. See how Riah's family does it. How they make sure to keep humans safe. Would you believe us then?"

Chapter Fifteen

An Existential Crisis

Riah had never been so angry with me as when I'd offered up the full moon to the Wilders.

He hardly spoke to me for three weeks, only occasionally making an appearance to get something or the other off his chest.

First, it was how dare I suggest such a thing without running it by him first. But Owen's dad had clearly needed proof. He'd needed to witness something. And it's not like we'd had time to chat about it.

Second, it was to tell me I wasn't coming with, if that had been my aim. I didn't bother telling him what he already knew: that we were pretty much all going in the hopes that the trip turned into a planning session. Between Aubrin's family and however many of the brotherhood Owen's father managed to gather, we'd essentially be taking over Bayfield. My parents would be there, so I would be too.

Third, he'd sat in my chair and thoroughly drooped. "I'm terrified about you seeing me like that."

I knelt down in front of him. "Like what?"

"Before and after, Grace. I'm wild and rough, and generally struggle with an existential crisis each time."

"I killed my uncle," I reminded him. This was our current working theory. "I'm a walking existential crisis."

The fourth time he came to our room was the day we were leaving. By then, he must have come to terms with it because he pulled me against him and buried his face in my neck.

I wrapped my arms around him and held on tight.

Aubrin, Nehemiah, and the thirty members of her pack—or extended family, however you wanted to look at it—were coming directly from Richland Center. Mai was driving up with Owen, his parents, and the cells Mr. Wilder had reached out to, the ones willing to look us in the eye and not kill us on sight. My parents and I followed Riah's family up, and all of us converged on Bayfield about the same time.

When we arrived at the bed and breakfast we'd booked, it was locked up, looking closed for the season. When my mom went straight for the mat that hid the key, I cut a look at her.

My dad leaned over to me. "She knows a guy."

Like ants disrupted from their anthill, most of us spilled through the old mansion, checking out each room and the view of the bay. Mr. Jenkins started a fire and the brotherhood disappeared into the carriage house where they were staying for everyone's comfort.

After dinner, Owen and his dad joined us around the firepit, where I roasted marshmallows like any old normal even though it was February and cold enough to see your breath with every exhale. Mrs. Jenkins and Maribel purposely drank their meal there, sure to be seen not sinking their fangs into anyone's flesh.

Little by little, more of the brotherhood trailed out of the carriage house. They clustered together, arms crossed, and when it seemed like every one of them had joined us, I made my way over. Owen introduced me and I tried to remember them by cells but pretty soon my brain was muddled.

I'd wandered over for a purpose, though, so when the chatting died down, I asked Mr. Wilder, "What do you need out of this weekend? What can I do to help you make your decision?"

"I think we just need to see it," he said. "See that we can be in the same room as abnormals. See they're not all a threat. See how they manage life *not* being a threat."

I gazed across the fire at Mrs. Jenkins and Maribel. "They're drinking blood right now and not being a threat."

"Why are they so skinny?" one of the men asked. "It's kind of creepy."

Mrs. Wilder gave him an irritated look.

"They drink only what they need. The compulsion for blood

isn't about taste, so it's not like eating a bag of your favorite treat and not being able to put it down. It's purely for sustenance. But they say the more you drink—and the fresher you drink—the more you want it. So in Shady, they dole it out carefully to help quench the instinct, then think nothing more about it."

"What if someone wanted to try it fresh?" one of them asked. "What if they bit someone?"

"They'd get kicked out of town." This was stretching the truth a bit. But it didn't happen very often, and if a vampire couldn't get their urges under control, they would indeed get exiled.

"How do they get their blood?" another asked.

"The dendrites in town donate to the blood bank, which stores it for them to pick up."

"I'd donate," Mai piped up, from where she was tucked under Owen's arm. "Can I donate?"

"Sure." I smiled. "In a pinch, you can even cut yourself. You don't turn into a vampire yourself unless they bite you, and you don't die unless they drain you."

Her eyes widened a bit, but not with the same kind of thrilled wonder as was normal for her. Maybe the novelty was wearing off, and the reality of how dangerous we could be truly setting in.

"Well." I clapped my mittens together. "If you want to see them in their natural habitat so as to deem they aren't a threat, then I think it's time for some euchre."

I corralled everyone inside the big house and collected those who wanted to play, then Riah's sister Ava set up a tournament bracket.

We played for so long, so late into the night, that people started nodding off wherever they were sitting. Eventually, the brotherhood all retreated back to the carriage house and a few of Aubrin's family made their way upstairs. Tomorrow, when the wolves traveled further north for the deserted Apostle islands, there'd be more beds. But tonight, people curled on any chair or rug they could find.

⁓ele⁓

The next day, as the hours ticked closer to the full moon, Riah changed.

Not all at once, but little by little.

Normally, he'd say goodbye to me the day before the full moon or the morning he left, but in Bayfield, I got to witness how he grew more relaxed as the minutes ticked closer. He was slower and more languid in how he moved, but rougher with his tone and shorter with his words. A falling off, maybe, of his carefully cultivated humanity.

When it came time for the wolves to set up camp, we rode a few windsleds across the lake, a vehicle somewhere undecided between a plane and a boat, all the way to one of the furthest islands, far from where anyone lived year round.

By we, I meant all the wolves, Riah's mom and sister, Mr. Wilder's cell, and I.

The guys who were driving the windsleds were clearly wolves

as well, wide and burly with thick hair and bushy beards. Riah said they'd run us back to safety and rejoin them before the third stage of twilight.

While Mr. Jenkins explained to Mr. Wilder how the night would go, Riah clung to me, a silent and tortured goodbye.

I was still trying to sort through his expression on the way back, with Owen's dad standing next to me on the wind sled.

"They seem like stand-up guys," he muttered, tucking his chin into his scarf.

"They are," I agreed, considering if the look on Riah's face had simply been as close to wild as I'd ever seen him.

"This was smart, Grace, you inviting us along."

Jerking my glance away from the white expanse of frozen lake and sky, I asked, "Does that mean you'll help us?"

"On the surface, it looks worth preserving, yes."

I studied him. "Is there something you think we're hiding?"

"No." With a huff, he ran a gloved hand over his face. "It's just hard for me to trust something that's not..."

"Human?"

He nodded and stared off into the distance.

"My make-up is exactly like yours," I told him. "The only difference is that some intangible aspect of my brain works differently. I'll give you that the wolves, vampires, and sirens can't say the same, but they all have the necessary components. They have a brain, a heart, and a soul. And trust me when I say their potential for violence is no different than ours."

"But they have to choose not to be violent, which is a higher hurdle than choosing *to* be violent."

"Why do you think that?"

"It's instinct for them. How they were made. Humans weren't made with that instinct."

"Sure they were. Humans were made with the instinct to categorize and separate out those who are weaker than them, the instinct to persecute and torture those below them on the hierarchy in order to make sure they keep their place."

He assessed me. "That doesn't exactly translate to human violence."

"But it's what starts it, isn't it? I'll give you that an abnormal's violence stems from survival instinct, but that just means humans have less of an excuse. Human violence stems from hatred or fear; and it's a choice. It's not because their livelihood depends on it."

He pursed his lips, hopefully not because I'd upset him. Hopefully because he could see how right I was.

———ell———

Maribel woke me around three in the morning by bouncing on the edge of my bed.

"Is something wrong?" I asked.

"No." She beamed. "Look!" And she shoved her phone in my face, the screen shining so brightly I had to squint.

It took me a minute to make sense of what I was seeing, but as it clicked, my jaw dropped open. "Is that...?"

She nodded.

"Holy crap!" I grabbed for the phone and sat up, fully awake now and needing a better look at it.

"I only got one shot. As soon as he saw the flash, he charged me."

My head shot up with a gasp.

She laughed. "You should've seen how they moved. I wish I could send you the memory."

We sat staring at the screen of her phone. Instead of the variegated color pattern found on wolves in the wild, every strand of his fur was the exact same sandy brown as his hair. His ears were slightly larger and more pointed, and his snout longer and wider. Every time it would fade out, I'd turn it on again and check to make sure the picture was still there. Eventually, she settled down next to me under the covers.

"You didn't see him kill anything, did you?" I whispered.

She shook her head. "I've never ran faster, trying to get there in time. I should've timed myself, seriously."

"How can you be sure it's Riah?"

"I just knew. Maybe it wouldn't have been so easy if he weren't my triplet, but it felt like him. And look at his eyes."

They did look oddly the same, like though his entire body had shifted into something new, his eyes were still his own. I sent the picture to myself and handed Maribel her phone. She lay grinning at it for a while, but wandered back to her room before I fell fully back to sleep.

The next time I woke, it was to Riah slipping in the room at dawn.

His eyes were hooded and weary, yet something raw and powerful radiated off of him as he pulled his shirt over his head. He strode across the room bare-chested and crawled onto the bed, pants and socks still on. Settling next to me on his side, he wrapped an arm around me, the sheet and blankets a barrier between us.

Closing his eyes, he buried his nose in my hair, inhaling like it was the last breath he'd ever take, then burrowed his head into my neck to kiss my collarbone, leaving his lips pressed there for so long I thought he might have fallen asleep.

"Riah?"

"Yes?" His voice was husky and broken, like he'd been screaming at a concert. Or maybe, I realized, howling at the moon.

I wiggled a little to face him, which was difficult because he was holding onto me so tight, muscles locked. His eyelids fluttered and he looked at me, something in them reminding me more of the vicious creature in my phone than the boy I knew.

One of his hands was pressed firmly against my lower back, holding me to him or holding him to sanity, I couldn't tell. "Are you all right?"

"I could smell you the minute I came back to myself. Could smell that you'd been there. Could smell you all the way here, and could smell what room you were in, just like I was afraid of."

"But there was nothing to be afraid of, see?" I wanted to run my hands over his face and push his hair out of the way, but he had my arms trapped, so I kissed him, whatever skin I could reach.

"You say that without understanding the kind of restraint I'm showing right now, holding back so I don't crush you."

"You want to crush me?"

"No, I just... want to be closer to you. Need to."

"Then get under the covers, silly."

He blew his hair out of his face to better look at me. "I don't trust myself to get under the covers."

"But I do." I offered him a soft smile. "I trust you. And I've been right so far."

———ele———

By the time everyone was well and truly awake that morning, Mr. Wilder had transformed the kitchen into a command center. An intricately detailed map of our town was spread across the table, held down by discarded coffee mugs.

"This is what we know," he said. "But it's old and I'm sure it's changed a bit. We need to get more insight from you on how to get in, figure how we'll coordinate our attack, and then decide on when."

I picked up a pencil to sketch in the new development and the new Sentinel station as my mom looked over my shoulder and explained what I was drawing. Then, with a red pen, I drew in the tunnel, effectively handing over the best way to infiltrate town to our biggest enemy.

My palms did get a bit sweaty with that.

Finally, with a highlighter I had handy in my backpack, I marked the places we could position others from inside, and soon Mr. Jenkins and Mr. Wilder were well on their way to forming a solid plan.

Chapter Sixteen

Because of Me

Lanterns, torches, and flashlights peppered the tangled green space that was Wisconsin wilderness.

The lights and shadows played across all of Aubrin's family and a large chunk of the state's Hand members. These were the ones who had the least skin in the game. I swallowed hard as I took them all in, my throat thick with gratitude.

Nehemiah, Aubrin, Owen, Riah, Nate, and I stood in a little clump. Nate was so close to me, our shoulders touched. He, too, didn't care a lick about the town but refused to let me run into a fight without him.

The mass of us were silent, waiting, and when the single howl came that told us it was time, we streamed into the tunnels.

The plan was to converge on Shady from all directions while simultaneously taking over the council and Sentinel buildings. My brother and Clara and a few others who sympathized with us were on duty at the Sentinel's headquarters, and the old council was ready to breach to town hall.

The Alpha Court, who owed us for turning Samuel over a few years ago, had come in through the woods behind Riah's house and were waiting with Riah's mom and sisters. Any who were willing and able would join them in the streets.

The Elder Board had also agreed to help because we'd notified them when their predecessors had been killed in an attempted takeover. They, and the forty odd Vamguard they'd felt comfortable sparing from regular duty, would be heading in with Jeremy's family from the truck stop.

Aster, her mom, and my grandparents were congregated with a bunch of others at the movie theater under the ruse of nighttime entertainment. Our plan was, if necessary, to squeeze the violent out of Shady Woods like the inflamed oozing puss of an infection that it was.

The new council and their supporters definitely beat us in numbers, but we were hoping they wouldn't be expecting us, and that maybe the wilds and out-of-towners would flee once they realized what was happening. That to them, Shady wouldn't be worth the fight.

A hungry sort of rumbling rolled through the tunnels as so many feet padded along the soft dirt floor, and I imagined it might sound, above, like the belly of the town waking, shaking itself off, and demanding to be seen for what it was always meant to be.

Stella and Ethan had been scheduled to work and were waiting in the Parrino's cellar. Slipping over to them, we let the adults move past us up the stairs; the first and most experienced were to lead the charge. I introduced them to Owen and Aubrin. Owen nodded and shook Ethan's hand but very few words were exchanged.

When it was our turn to head up, I felt for the axe strapped to my waist, as if it might have gone somewhere, then patted down my pockets which were stuffed with peeled garlic.

Robby and the rest of the staff were waiting in the bar, motioning people over to vats of bright yellow paint tinged with siren tears that sat along the dark cherry wood. To mark which side we were on, we sunk an arm in, fingertips to elbow, then swiped it across our foreheads. This would keep us from attacking each other.

Stepping out into the night, we were greeted with a dendrite-spread announcement that I knew was being cast far and wide to reach anyone in town limits:

Old Shady has taken the town hall and the Sentinel station.

This pacifist town is no place for anyone but those who choose to live a peaceful life.

Embrace old Shady or leave promptly.

A few more howls echoed across the night, which meant it had started; a fight was on.

The moment I might have killed my uncle came speeding back to me, slamming against my chest. What it felt like to think I'd taken a life, and that I might have to do it again.

It felt terribly not pacifist, but I'd expected this might turn into kill or be killed. No time to think on it now.

It seemed everyone, friend and foe, had converged at the main intersection. Fighting had already spilled past the bank and pharmacy, and was leaking toward the general store. Riah held me back as long as he could, as long as the adults seemed to have it under control, as long as there weren't too many for them. Eventually, though, he had to jump in, which meant I did the same.

Owen took a wild vampire's head off with a blade somewhere between a knife and a sword, and the viscous purple blood splattered him from nearly head to toe.

I copied his arc, since we were about the same height, and tried my axe out on the first vicious wolf that came at me. It sunk into his soft flesh like it might a raw breast of chicken, knocked into bone, and nearly took me down as he fell.

I wrenched it out of where it had split his collarbone and was left standing in shock over his dead body at how quickly he'd fallen.

Sure, Jeremy had sharpened my axe for me, said it was lethal, but killing someone should not be that easy.

My stomach rolled and it was all I could do not to vomit on him, managing instead to empty the contents of my stomach onto the pavement next to him. I straightened just in time to sidestep a vampire, eyes glassy with lunacy and mouth drooling with the hope of my taste on his lips.

I swung haphazardly, hoping for any contact at all, which only lobbed his hand off and made him angrier. Flying back at me, vampire fast, he caught my neck with his other hand, squeezing until my breaths came out in wheezes, then a whistle, then nearly nothing at all.

Shutting my eyes tight, I wondered where all my instincts had gone, all the hours I'd spent training. The axe in my hand had me thinking like an axe-thrower instead of a fighter.

Could I somehow be the fighter, but with an axe in my hand?

Just when I was about to drop my weapon so I could better fight him off before I passed out, his head exploded across my face and he collapsed in a lump on the ground.

Thanks, Nate, I said, gasping for air and stuffing a garlic clove into the wound to make sure it didn't heal itself.

No problem, kid.

I was in a sea of writhing, vicious strangers.

Riah shattered the face of a vampire coming at me with his fist, then slammed a clove of garlic into her mouth.

Owen's arm stopped the teeth of a wolf, and with the wild attached there, I sliced through his neck. Then we had the little problem of a wolf head attached to Owen's arm.

He gave me a look. I gave him one back. Riah stepped in and pried the teeth apart, using the head to whack a werewolf coming at us. The head bounced away, and Riah sunk his fingers into the momentarily stunned wolf's neck to pull his throat out.

Owen's now bloody arm came out in front of me again, trying to protect me from a vampire I thought I recognized from the blood bank, her fangs out and eyes on my neck. Before she reached us, she was shot in the head.

Nate and that gun.

I didn't have time to think about how good his aim was. I was fighting for my life and needing a lot of help. Holding the axe up closer to its blade, I tried to accommodate for its weight, thinking of it like an extension of my arm instead of something I had to wind up and throw. Stepping over bodies, I sunk my weapon into what I had to believe was evil, over and over again.

Or was I evil—were we all evil—for being there in the first place?

At some point, the crowd thinned. When only a few remained and they realized they were alone, they took off.

I gaped at the scattered bodies on the pavement, the street-lamps casting softly slanting light across twisted limbs and gory wounds. It was a movie set. Not real.

It couldn't be real.

My mom checked in with us all collectively, and my brother assured us all that he and Clara were all right.

A body twitched to the right of me and I turned into Riah, my face landing in something wet and surely disgusting. I didn't care; I was in shock. Burying my face in someone's entrails was better than facing what we'd done.

Jeremy came stalking through the mess, prodding bodies with the flat side of his axe to check for any injured who might need help. I could only stare at the wicked cut across his cheek and the torn shirt that gaped open in the breeze. It also looked like he might be missing a few fingers.

When he finally spotted us, he moved vampire fast to wrap his arms around me and kiss me on the forehead. Then Stella, Ethan and Riah, even Owen, who only slightly furrowed his brow at the contact.

Grace, is Nate with you? my mom asked. *He's not answering.*

Spinning in a circle, I searched for his wheat blond hair and the stupid hoody he always wore.

Nate! Shoving away from my friends, I stumbled through the street, turning bodies that were face down and checking detached heads.

What I found was Christian, blinking up into the night, his shirt soaked with blood.

Dropping to my knees, I clasped his hand and called for Stella; I called for his dad, his mom, Nora, Robby, any other sirens I knew who might be close, Aster and Jeremy to let them know, even Sofia. I didn't know if she was around, if she was even in Shady anymore, or which side she might have been fighting on, but figured, in case she wanted to say goodbye.

No.

There would be no goodbyes.

Hang on, Chris. I've got you.

Everyone converged at once. Stella, skidding to a stop. Jeremy right behind her. Aster from the other direction. His dad, in my head, trying to make his way to us.

Stella was already teary-eyed and motioned for Riah to rip his shirt open so she could try to heal his wound. When it was revealed, though, she only gaped at it, as one tear slipped down her cheek. "It's so big. I don't think I can... I don't think this will work." Still, she leaned over him and tried, pouring her essence into him.

I had a dream about this, he muttered, his voice weak. *You saved me.* He squeezed my hand, pulling my attention from his chest to his face. *You always save me.*

How'd I save you? Tears dripped down my cheeks and off my chin. *Tell me what to do.*

Seal my skin with your fingers.

I shook my head—he clearly had no idea how split open he was—and screamed for his dad as the silver flecks in his eyes seemed to fade. Weakly, Christian lifted my hand to drag it along his wound, then went limp, his head dropping to the side.

Rage and grief welled up inside me and I wanted to scream. I had to scream. I let it out, and as I did, blue sparks also erupted from my fingers. My tears dried as I stared at them, and suddenly I knew what he meant.

"Hold his skin together," I told Stella, as she lifted up from the gash that was now full of a churning, molten silver.

"What?"

"Hold his skin together!"

She placed a palm on either side and pressed together, but couldn't get the skin to meet, only succeeding in pushing some of the siren tears out. Forehead creased, she looked up at me.

"Try starting at one end. We'll work from one side to the other. His skin has to touch, so I can... so I can cauterize it."

Stella raised an eyebrow but did as she was told.

Little by little, we sealed him back up. Just as it was done, his parents found us and his dad took over, taking stock of where his nurses were and how to get Christian to his clinic. That's when I remembered Nate.

I staggered to my feet. Aster caught me.

"Nate," I explained, letting myself lean against her for a moment.

"Go," she told me. "We'll stay with Christian."

As I flew over bodies and slid through blood, checking face after face after face, I promised God that if Nate lived, I'd never fight again. I'd stand down. They could take Shady, they could take the state, they could take the country—the world—and I would stand down.

I would take whatever they gave me, I'd take injury and torture and death, before hurting anyone else, if only Nate was still here with us.

Nate! My brother was calling for him too. Clara and my parents, all of us searching.

I found Aster's parents, and Riah's, and Maribel, all alive. I found Aubrin, and Owen's dad, everyone searching for their people. I found Jeremy's parents, and I found mine.

Then I spotted my brother and knew.

Justin stood beneath a streetlamp in front of the bank, head hung and body still. Clara was looking at the same thing he was, her hand on his back.

I don't know how I made it the rest of the way there, but I did. When I caught sight of my cousin, however, my knees gave out. My brother caught me, turned me into him, and held me tight.

He was shaking. Or sobbing. Or I was. I couldn't tell.

Nate had been swiped nearly through, a deep cut across his belly. His face was pasty and vapid, as if he were already in a casket.

He was here because of me. He was *dead* because of me.

I would never forgive myself.

Chapter Seventeen

A List of Names

The next day's paper was nothing but a list of names.

It hit the doorstep late, after noon, when I'd just woken up and forced myself down the stairs. Forced, because though Shady had hopefully been righted, everything else felt very, very wrong.

I opened the front door to a lovely, late March sun, and realized that spring break would now, forever and always, be nothing to me but a time to mourn.

Picking up the paper, my blurry eyes scanned the pages, unable to focus.

I knew Nate Jameson would be on the list and I couldn't face it. I couldn't face Ava Jenkins either. Seeing their names in print would make it too hard to breathe. Not that they weren't already haunting me in my sleep.

Still, to honor the dead, I wiped my eyes, closed the door, and moved for the kitchen table. If it took me all day, I would read every name on that list.

Eric Parrino.

Layla Parrino.

Caroline from work.

So many of my classmates, so many of my neighbors, so *many*.

My tears dropped onto the newsprint.

A hand loosened my fingers from the paper, pulled it across the table, and sat down next to me. I wiped my eyes clear and Owen's face registered.

He reached for my hand and squeezed. "I'm terribly sorry for your loss."

I stared at him through an empty, black tunnel of grief. "This is all my fault."

"Life isn't your fault, Grace. Which means death isn't either." Settling back, he took the coffee mug my grandma handed him. I wasn't sure where she'd come from, or if she'd been there all along. I'd not been paying attention to much after I grabbed that newspaper off the stoop.

Mr. Wilder had lost a few of his men, but not his son. Or, maybe I should say, not his other son. I had to tell them about Todd before they left. I'd promised myself I would.

Our house was full of the brotherhood. It was the only place they felt comfortable sleeping, and no one had left town last night after the battle. No one who wasn't fleeing for good.

Aster's mom was hosting the Alpha Court at her house, and the Parrino's had the Elder Board at theirs. Riah's neighborhood had absorbed Aubrin's family, and the Vamguard had camped out around Jeremy's house.

My dad walked in the front door and I blinked at him, not even realizing he'd been gone.

"The new council is nowhere to be found," he reported, making a beeline for my grandma and the cup of coffee she was pouring for him. "Well, about a third of them are dead, but the rest are MIA. The Sentinel they've rounded up are all on our side, and can all be vouched for. Your mom awake?"

I shook my head and he headed up the stairs. Owen's dad appeared, leaning against the entry to the kitchen, and when he didn't move from there, my grandma walked coffee to him.

If my heart hadn't been chewed up and left in pieces, I would've smiled that she was compelled to provide this weak comfort, even when knowing no true comfort could be had.

"Mr. Wilder." I cleared my throat. "Would you please sit down?"

"You don't need to thank us, Grace. We're proud to have fought alongside you. I don't regret it."

I took a deep breath and nodded to the chair next to Owen. He took it.

Might as well rip the band-aid off, right? "Todd is alive."

Owen choked on his swig of coffee, to which my grandma patted his back, and Mr. Wilder blinked.

"His cell tried to burn our town four years ago. They'd imagined we'd scatter and planned to hunt us." I looked down at the scuffed wood table and ran my fingers along its curved edge. "As it were, Riah and I were right in the middle of it. But they're not dead."

"Where are they?" Owen asked, and as I peeked up at him, I caught his dad's stare. "Are they injured? Are they here?"

I shook my head. "We gave them a siren tear potion to wipe their memory and split them up. We dropped Todd and Rick in Tennessee to start a new life."

"That's..." Mr. Wilder struggled to contain himself, tears filling his eyes. "Well, it's not bad news."

"Will they know us?" Owen asked, his face white.

"No. They won't know anything of this life anymore. But I'll tell you where they are. Or where we left them anyway." I swallowed, feeling like I was betraying my people for theirs, but they deserved it, after what they'd done for us.

Mr. Wilder shook his head. "I don't understand. I'd told him, time and again, that Shady was last on our list."

"Maybe he took that to mean we were an easy get," my grandma suggested, a note of bitterness in her voice.

Gram, I warned.

She gave me a petulant look. *You should have told me ahead of time if you didn't want me to react.*

Mr. Wilder swallowed hard. "Is he happy there?"

I shrugged one shoulder. "We haven't checked on them."

"Dad. If Todd's alive, he can take your place."

"I don't want him to take my place." Mr. Wilder squeezed his son's shoulder. "You were always the one with a good head on your shoulders, it's why I was so hard on you. It was frustrating watching you grow, knowing you could take over, if only you had a little of Todd's fortitude. But he was all fortitude and no discernment." His eyes flickered to my grandma. "It's *not* about hatred."

I realized then that the brotherhood was about protecting their way of life just like we wanted to protect ours. Live and let live, but for those who weren't going to let you live, then watch out.

Chapter Eighteen

Wanna See a Wolf?

By the time the end of the summer rolled around, Shady felt like itself again.

It had settled so much, in fact, that we were bringing Owen and Mai home with us. Owen because I wanted him to see proof of what it had all been for, and Mai because she'd been begging to see this 'magical place—*what a dream*—like a fairytale come to life.'

Not that I'd ever seen a vampire in a fairytale.

We stopped at the truck stop on the way in, and I grinned as we rolled into the lot, which was vacant, exactly as it should be.

Mai squealed with delight the moment she was through the door, even though this truck stop presented the same as any other. The only difference was the axe display, but she veered right past that to Jeremy, who sat on a stool behind the counter.

"Do you remember me?" she asked. They'd had dinner together when Aster and Jeremy had visited us in Madison. When we'd found out Owen was brotherhood, thanks to his tattoo.

"What I remember is you're human." Jeremy shook his head, then let out an exasperated sigh. "Only Grace would bring a human to town. Twice."

I stuck my tongue out at him as Mai beamed. "Can I see your teeth?" she asked.

Jeremy clicked them out and Mai nearly melted. He grinned. "You know I'm not just some object to adore, right? I'm a person too."

"I'm in love with you," she stated. "Can I have your number?"

"All right, slow down," Owen tugged her away from the counter and slid a few candy bars toward the register. "He's the only vampire you've ever met."

"That I know of!" she cried, then bounced back through the store. "I cannot *believe* this is happening to me. *Dream* vacay."

"Might be the only, but I can also guarantee I'm the best," Jeremy said as he rang Owen up. "Sure you don't want an axe?"

"Maybe next time."

"They're great souvenirs. I whittle them myself."

"You *whittle?*" I laughed. "You're a *whittler?*"

"You know very well I carve axes, Grace James. And it's been very quiet around here. What else am I supposed to do with my time?"

"Quiet is good," Riah reminded.

"Quiet is very good," Jeremy agreed.

Mai stood at the window now, surveying the back of the lot where the blacktop was pretty broken up. Dilapidated for show, but really turning itself into the gravel road that would take us into the woods and straight to Shady. Her hands were on her hips and she was beaming from ear to ear.

Nora patted the counter. "We'll see you later, Jer. Time to make someone's dreams come true."

———ℓℓ———

We drove past the Sentinel station where four men in uniform were playing cards at a picnic table out front. They waved as we drove by and Nora pointed out the blood bank for Mai.

She begged us to stop, but Nora reminded her this wasn't a zoo. I told her I'd see if Dr. Riley would let us in his basement to see the animals, and that we could take her to the window and the attic and the cooler.

If she behaved herself, Nora added.

I refrained from suggesting Nora bring her to the bottom of the lake for a stop in Iara. We could save that mind-blowing experience for another time.

Of all the restaurants in town, Mai wanted to go to Parrino's most. Al's was a close second, but it didn't have a cellar, and the bloody drinks and dishes on Parrino's menu intrigued her more than Al's offerings of raw meat. Not that any of us were surprised. Her first love was the vampire, after all.

It was a busy Friday night, so while we waited for a table in the pizza pit, I brought her downstairs to meet to Constantine. As we stood at his bar, she stared down the Parrino trios he was prepping. Grabbing one of the shots, she downed Constantine's sloth and tortoise mixture.

I wrinkled my nose. She turned to me and wrinkled hers as well.

"That's not going to do anything for you," Riah said.

Her shoulders dropped. "How do I become a vampire?"

Constantine raised an eyebrow as Riah and I both said, emphatically, "You don't."

Next, we brought her into the kitchen and introduced her to Ethan, Stella, Robby, and Jack. She asked them all if they were vampires, and Robby assured her he was better than a vampire.

"I'm a siren," he said.

Mai waved her hand, unimpressed. "Yeah, I know a siren."

Jack lost it. He was laughing so hard, he turned red and started coughing. We left them for our table, which finally ready, just as Christian walked in.

He beamed at me, which is what he did now, and took a few quick strides to gather me up in a tight embrace.

"My angel," he muttered. I wiggled out of his arms as Riah rolled his eyes, jealous that this was a thing and probably would be forever.

"It was nothing," I said, for the millionth time. "You literally saved yourself by telling me what to do."

His gaze settled on Mai. "Who's this?"

"A friend of ours from school."

"A friend like Aubrin?" he asked.

"No. A friend like Charlie."

Chris huffed out a short laugh. "Wow. Full circle, that."

A silence settled as those of us who were there for Charlie's visit remembered those days. Before all the chaos. Or, I guess, the start of the chaos.

When the pause stretched a bit heavy, and likely uncomfortably for Mai, she asked Christian brightly, "So, what are you?"

I winced, though I'd done the exact same thing to Riah when I'd met him.

Wow was right. Full, complete circle.

"Dendrite." Then he pointed to his eyes. "With a splash of siren. Did you know Grace saved my life?"

She shook her head. At school, we did not talk about that night.

Christian lifted up his shirt to show her the char marks from my fingertips that still hadn't faded. "This was a gash a mile wide."

Mai's eyes widened and Christian winked. "Well, I'm just here to pick up takeout." He reached out to clasp Riah's hand. "Will I see you all before you leave?"

And then—you're not going to believe this—Sofia stalked up in the white and black ensemble that dubbed her one of the Parrino's waitstaff.

My jaw dropped.

"Close your mouth, dear," she said.

"No one told me you were working here."

"Shocker that you're not the center of everyone's universe?" she asked.

I grinned large, then told Mai, "She's a vampire," because there was nothing Sofia hated more than someone shiny and bubbly vomiting cheer all over her. And she had to take it, because she was the waitress.

Customer's always right, I reminded, lest she forget, and she sent me a tight smile, her nostrils flaring in irritation.

Aster joined us late and, watching Mai coo over Sofia all meal, eventually leaned over to Mai. "This vampire obsession is unnatural. Wanna see a wolf?"

Mai glanced at Riah. "I see a wolf every day."

"No. I mean, a *were*wolf." She tapped the screen of my cell alive, revealing the shot of Riah that Maribel had taken. Which I hadn't shown him yet.

Well, he'd probably seen it and thought it was off the internet or something.

Mai's mouth dropped open. "Is that you?" she asked Aster.

"It's Riah. On a full moon." Aster pulled up a shot of a real wolf on her phone and set them side by side to point out how you could tell the difference, but I was only paying attention to Riah's sharp intake of breath and steady exhale.

"Grace?"

"Yes?"

"Is that true?"

"Would you think I'd have another werewolf on my lock

screen?"

He snatched my phone from the table. "Tell me right now you didn't take this picture." Soft but certain panic filled his voice.

Sliding a hand on his knee, I replied, "You think I'd be alive right now if I tried to take a picture of a werewolf?"

"That's not funny." He ground his teeth together. "Don't even say that."

"You don't remember?" I asked gently, curious more than anything else.

"Of course I don't remember," he snapped.

Scooting my chair closer to him, I wrapped my arms around his neck and kissed the line of his jaw.

"Maribel came back in one piece," I told him. *Mostly.*

He tensed at that but I only laughed. It was over and past, the horror of her missing the tip of her finger. All of the horror, really. And we were all in one piece.

We'd go back to school next week and start our second year of college, knowing home was safe and sound and waiting for us.

A complete full circle, indeed.

Also By J Mercer

Contemporary young adult novels

Triplicity

Perfection and Other Illusive Things

In One Life and Out Another

Reviews really do make the world go round. Please let others know what you thought about A Brighter Day and the Shady Woods series!

Milton Keynes UK
Ingram Content Group UK Ltd.
UKHW050023250324
439966UK00014BA/907